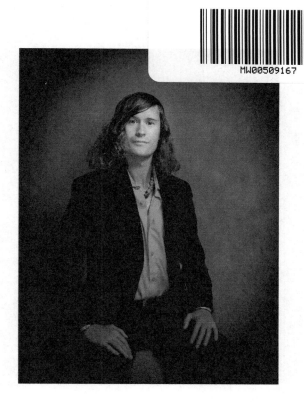

About the Author

Jonathan Wade Barrow has a Bachelor of Science degree in Communication from The University of Tennessee, Knoxville. Having lived in Hawaii and the Caribbean, he is an island lover with a passion for the ocean.

The Seraphic Songs of Satellite's Soul

Jonathan Wade Barrow

The Seraphic Songs of Satellite's Soul

Olympia Publishers
London

www.olympiapublishers.com
OLYMPIA PAPERBACK EDITION

A CIP catalogue record for this title is available from the British Library.

ISBN: 978-1-80074-325-0

This is a work of fiction.
Names, characters, places and incidents originate from the writer's imagination. Any resemblance to actual persons, living or dead, is purely coincidental.

First Published in 2023

Olympia Publishers
Tallis House
2 Tallis Street
London
EC4Y 0AB
Printed in Great Britain

Acknowledgements

A very great thanks to Sherleen, Savannah, and all the strong seraphs of our beautiful Earth.

Chapter

Chapter 1 The Turquoise Tiger Tooth 11

Chapter 2 Meeting the Idens 23

Chapter 3 Coasting Along the Coast 35

Chapter 4 Swashbuckle At Starnectar 47

Chapter 5 Smile of My Mind's Eye 59

Chapter 6 JettySet's Alma Mater 72

Chapter 7 Voyaging Full Volume 82

Chapter 8 The Erusaexel Suit 95

Chapter 9 Zooming Through the Music Video Shoot 107

Chapter 10 The Hottest Globe Trot to Ever Drop 121

Chapter 11 The Seraph 139

Chapter 1
The Turquoise Tiger Tooth

"Satellite, have you had breakfast yet?" Grandmother called softly over the room-to-room intercom. It was early morning aboard Lexeasure, the ice white superyacht. Lexeasure was the pride and joy of Satellite's granddad. Granddad had acquired the yacht after the success of his technology company Omnikinetica.

It was the summer of Satellite's eighteenth birthday, and her grandparents had offered her a job at their new for-fun startup company, Lilikoi Source. Lilikoi Source had its home in Kauai, but it was aboard the Lexeasure that the magic happened. Fully equipped with a science lab, Satellite's granddad cultivated lilikoi vines to thrive in different climates, and then shipped seed orders around the world.

"I'll have the spicy tuna!" Satellite sang from her room into the intercom. Over the speaker, from the deck below, Satellite heard Grandmother open the refrigerator.

Making her bed, Satellite tossed her sun-soaked ocean tousled hair to one side, glancing in the mirror as she did so. There was a raw purity to her that shone all over her primed teenage body.

Her reflection winked, and she slipped into her emerald green bikini. The emerald pop beneath her fire red hair was stunning. The tips were blonded from days spent playing outside, but the volume was cherry red. Satellite strode straight across her spacious room and swung open the hatch to the vaulted hallway beyond.

"Breakfast!" Satellite had a great day ahead of her. She sat at the galley table as Grandmother brought over a bowl of rice with spicy tuna on top.

"Eat up, deary," Grandmother cooed. Satellite wolfed right into the ahi bowl; she was going to pick the plumpest lilikoi from the orchard today as model specimens for Granddad's lab. Her basket lay waiting atop the table, kerchief tucked inside.

"I bet you'll have some good lilikoi to snack on," Grandmother said with nurturing warmth.

Satellite nodded above the ahi bowl she had just wolfed down. "Just make sure you're back for supper, we're having crab cakes tonight."

Satellite touched her tongue to the top of her lips cheekily. "See you!" she chimed, and grabbing her basket, she marched barefoot out of the galley, through the spacious salon, and out across the pool deck to her fourteen-foot sailboat fastened to the back of the moored yacht's dock.

Untying the knots that held the sailboat in place, Satellite hopped aboard, looping the basket to the mast. "Find the plumpest ones!" breezed her Granddad's voice from the open doorway of the yacht's dock.

"Aye, aye," Satellite waved back. Pulling the ropes, she tightened the sails, catching the wind, and started skimming the ocean's surface towards shore about a quarter of a mile away.

She smiled from ear to ear as she sailed; the water had never looked so clear. The sight of the shore from the sea looked like a picture of what heaven must be. "A crown of mountains, that's what it looks like," Satellite thought to herself. The jagged, fluted range of the Na Pali Coast had been called the "center of the universe" before. It was here that the original Lilikoi Source test vines resided.

Catching a wave, Satellite surfed the sailboat sleekly onto the shore. Looking up at the view in front of her, Satellite wore a shiekish look on her featured face. She pulled the sailboat up onto the shelly sand, and loosening the cord that was around the mast, she grabbed her basket.

The beach was a veritable paradise. The sand itself was made of little bits of shells. Palm trees swayed, waterfalls rushed, and breezes whipped up from the beach to the fluted mountains. The life of the place was something else. It was music. The grass was so green, the rocks so smooth, the water so fresh. It was just so lush.

Satellite soaked up the scene as she found the path and began making her way towards the verdant valley. The path was earthen and jungly, and as it trailed into the valley, more and more wonderful and exotic plants lined it. A gentle river streamed alongside the path, at times revealing beautiful pools.

After a while on the path, Satellite reached a clearing. It was here that Granddad's Lilikoi Source vines lay nestled between the thick of the jungle and the rush of the river.

Satellite put her basket atop her elbow and began walking along the lined rows of lilikoi, her eyes flowing amongst the vines seeking out the plumpest fruits.

Granddad's breeding of the lilikoi had resulted in an abundant diversity in the growth style of the fruits. Some were petite and tart, others large and succulent. Satellite savored her time spent amongst the fertile grounds of the deep valley. There was a revelatory solitude in this place, she thought as she plucked a particularly plump lilikoi from a slender vine snaked around a sapling. The sunlight was different here. There was a tangible timelessness to it.

Satellite placed her now full basket in the shamrock strewn grass and alit atop a big boulder, sitting cross-legged, the fragrance of the rainforest lulling her into a happy trance.

She took a ripe lilikoi from the basket, and placing her thumbs together in the middle, popped the lilikoi open, with light purple juices spilling out over her fingers. She lifted the lilikoi up, took a look at the sun, and then graciously slurped into the lilikoi's tender and tart interior.

Her eyelids fluttered a little as the sweet nectar poured into her mouth, spilling over her tastebuds and dribbling down her chin. These, she thought, looking at the chewy seeds inside, were a microcosm form of the universe. Like a small version of something much larger. Gathering herself together, Satellite clasped a grasp on the basket handle, and plucking a last lilikoi from a vine, she stepped back onto the valley path.

Having collected the lilikoi Granddad needed for the lab, she peered through the dense jungle to where the beach lay. She kept a camera in a compartment of her sailboat and wanted to capture a few pictures of barreling waves for her album before sunset.

Busy thoughts walked with her along the path, where her imagination played in the pools and palm trees that ran alongside the neat jungle course.

As she rounded a moss-covered boulder, she noticed a tiny trail that meandered over to a small sunlit garden maze. Satellite stepped off the valley path and onto the narrow trail that was only wide enough for one foot at a time.

Tracing the narrow trail over to the sunlit garden maze,

Satellite let out a gentle gasp. There was a stone pillar at the center, where, glinting in the subdued light through the jungle canopy, a turquoise tiger tooth necklace was hung invitingly.

The jungle, having been silent for a while, now seemed to be filled with the songs of hundreds of tropical birds. Satellite gazed from the narrow trail to the symmetrical entrance of the miniature maze, smiling to the chirping chaos above.

The maze was lined with beautiful full ferns, and as Satellite followed the little labyrinth's grassy grooves, a warm gravity seemed to gently press in on her from all sides.

A soft and rapturously melodic epiphany extracted itself from the garden maze and attached itself to her as she reached the center point. Satellite's eyes sparkled as the jungle rippled around her. The moment was heavy, she realized. This place was special. Small bugs drifted lazily in the barely present jungle breeze.

Satellite swiftly nipped down to the turquoise tiger tooth. She deftly lifted the back of the necklace up and over the stone pillar. A momentary flash popped into her mind, a vision of the inside of some sort of immaculate facility. Young figures with stark straight postures dressed in all white uniforms marched in formation in her mind. Startled by the clarity and force of the vision, Satellite stood up, raptly at attention, raising the necklace up above her head where it caught a ray of sunlight, the fine details of it illuminated.

Staring awe-struck at the beautiful turquoise tiger tooth which adorned a handsome silver chain, Satellite unclipped the fastener and lightly swung the jewelry around her neck and atop her youthful shoulders. Visions of white uniformed young figures marching inside a facility now seemed to be playing like a movie in the back of her mind.

Ecstatic with the magic of her newfound treasure, Satellite let out a whispered squeal of delight, her now clenched fists trembling in pleasure. Spinning on the spot, she smoothly glided along the grooves of the garden maze, exiting the little labyrinth with an elated look shining on her breath-taking face.

Along the narrow trail and back onto the valley path, Satellite marched in the direction of the beach, daydreams dancing behind her eyes. Just to the side of the path, the rocks that riddled the rushing river acted as stepping stones to a deep pool.

Satellite sprinted across the tops of the rocks and slipped into the cool water. A moment of submersion, then Satellite burst out of the pool. Her toned body guided rivulets of sparkling streams in clean reams as her tight emerald bikini glistened against the vibrancy of her solar flare hair.

Rejuvenated, she took off into a sprint down the path, sopping drops of water in all directions. She could see the beach now up ahead through the thick underbrush and zigzagging path. Squashing a few fallen mangoes beneath her bare feet, she felt the juice squelch through her toes, and, now energetically sprinting, she clutched her basketful of lilikoi.

"Fwoosh!" Emerging from the jungle, Satellite stood atop a grassy knoll where the wind was sweeping the scene. In front of her was the gently sloping side of the grassy knoll, followed by a wet grassy field which led to a short path down and along a seaside cliff, where, finally, the beautiful beach sprawled out on the shoreline.

Lightly jogging now, Satellite followed the cliff top path as it wound its way down to the shoreline where her sailboat stood out as the only sign of presence on the primordial nature of this remote beach. In the distance, the refraction of the many windows of the Lexeasure reflected the stunning mountainous coastline, shining; a true beacon of home.

Rounding the final bend, Satellite's jog turned to a walk as she made her way across a grass field that was so green, she bounced a little with dance as she looked it all over. Passing the edge of the field, she hopped across a few boulders that were half buried in the shelly sand, and with one final hop, Satellite stood shoulders back, chest out, on the awesome expanse of the beach.

The shelly sand stretched on for what could be the size of a stadium. Out and away, it felt as if the beach was a stage with the crown-like mountains poised as a humongous amphitheater. The space, the incredible sense of space was phenomenal.

Satellite, her feet sinking into the sand with each step, trod across the expanse towards her sailboat. The horizon seemed massive here. Thoughts running wild, combined with the visions of the turquoise tiger tooth, culminated in what seemed to be the most alive she had ever felt.

Reaching her sailboat, Satellite plopped the basket of lilikoi down next to the compartment where she kept her camera. Opening the compartment, she brought out the camera which was housed in a waterproof case. The sun glimmered on her tanned skin as she turned the camera on and looked at the ocean. A large barreling wave folded from left to right, just offshore.

Smile lined up with the horizon, Satellite dashed down the beach, camera in hand, and dove into the face of a wave. Swimming easily around, she caught the next wave, sticking her camera hand up and snapping a picture in the barreling tube. She played for hours, firing off tube shots as great waves came along, bodysurfing left and right, up and down. She writhed her supple body in the foamy whitewash, reveling in the grandeur.

As the sun set above the waters where she played in the amphitheater of the mountains, Satellite emerged, shimmering like the silhouette of an angel. Thinking of rinsing off, she glanced up and over at the waterfall that gushed down off the rocks of a beach front cliff. She darted up for a quick dunk, feeling quite spunky as she let the waterfall plunge itself on her right there on the beach front.

Satisfied, she bounded back to her boat, and winking to herself, she closed the camera back in its compartment and pushed off from the sand and into the ocean. She'd shower in her beautiful bathroom back on board Lexeasure before dinner, or maybe after, since they were having crab cakes tonight. Clambering onto her sailboat, she grabbed hold of the ropes and caught the wind, boosting up and over the breaking waves.

Glancing back, the sun had freshly set, and stars had appeared in the sky above the mountains. She felt accomplished having gathered the best lilikoi for Granddad, discovered what seemed to be a magical necklace, and having snapped fantastic shots of tubes for her album.

Focusing now on Lexeasure, she eased the sails out a bit as she was already near the ship. The aroma of Grandmother's crab cakes floated over and found Satellites nostrils. For the second time today, her eyelids fluttered in ecstasy.

Rearing the small sailboat to the right, she brought the boat around to the Lexeasure's dock. Granddad stood there, happy as a clam, waiting for her.

"How'd ya do?" He asked as she bumped up to the dock

platform.

"Plucked the plumpest ones!" Satellite said stepping onto the dock of Lexeasure, proudly displaying her packed basket.

"Well done," smiled Granddad, gently placing his hand on her back. "Put your basket in the galley and wash up, dinner's almost ready." Together they tied the sailboat to the dock and headed up the stairs.

Padding barefoot across the pool deck, the two entered the salon, making their way betwixt the book laden coffee table and the clean conceptual couches that were coddled in cushions.

Onward and out of the salon they went, through one of the two arched openings that connected to the galley where a warmly lit porthole window shone. Above the arched opening read the sign, "Grand's Galley". Turning the handle, the hatch unlatched, and pushing it open, a plethora of activity met their senses.

There grandmother was, up to her elbows at every countertop with culinary creations. And there the crab cakes were, lying deliciously on a large plate. Homemade cocktail sauce had been stirred in a dish, and there was garlic bread beside the corn on the cob. Some pickles and olives sat nicely on a shapely glass plate next to the banana pudding.

"Come in, come in you two," Grandmother said looking over the glasses of lilikoi kombucha tea at Satellite and Granddad. "Satellite, you're as salty as the sea; oh well, help me set the table and let's eat. I want to hear all about your day."

Satellite placed her full basket on a clear space on the counter and picked up the crab cake plate, moving to the table.

After a few bustling moments in which Granddad sampled a little bit of everything, they were seated at the galley table which was full of steaming supper entrees. Beaming at each other over the tops of the beautiful spread, Grandmother and Granddad looked at each other, then at Satellite, "Tuck in," they chorused in unison.

Satellite held their loving gaze, clapped her still sea spray covered hands together in prayer, and then the three of them nipped on in.

Grandmother's cooking was simply superb. Satellite tried adding some manners and grace, but she couldn't help but wolf down a cocktail sauce covered crab cake. Tasting this and that, chomping here and there, sipping delicious homemade lilikoi kombucha tea all the while, the delectable dinner lasted well into the late evening.

As she ate, Satellite recounted the tale of her adventures. Grandmother and Granddad listened with great attention amidst the description that Satellite characterized her story with. Pleased to hear that the vines in the valley were abundantly producing varieties of his specially bred lilikoi, Granddad's eyes and ears perked up when the story reached the narrow trail that had led to the small garden maze.

"And there it was, just hanging on the center point pillar?" inquired Granddad, his curiosity piqued at the turquoise tiger tooth that now adorned Satellite.

"Someone placed it there as a gift, I suppose," Satellite said. "It's definitely been illuminated by someone," Satellite continued, "I feel like I can see into it a little."

Grandmother and Granddad nodded at each other. They too were collectors of illuminated objects; Granddad's lab was populated with troves of trappings he had discovered on his travels.

"It's been gifted to you now, deary," Grandmother said,

smiling with wisdom, "May it grant unto you that which is endowed in it." An appreciative moment bubbled around the table; then, with one last spoonful of banana pudding and a swig of lilikoi tea, Satellite folded her napkin in closure. "Thank you for such a wonderful dinner," Satellite's voice was full and warm.

"Oh, before you go," Granddad started, "I'm going into Hanalei tomorrow morning for some supplies, would you like to come along?"

"Would I?" Satellite sang. She got up from the table and threw her arms around Granddad.

"I'll take that as a yes," Granddad said, chest swelling with cheer.

Dreams dancing all over, Satellite flitted over to Grandmother and kissed her cheek. "Make sure you're up at dawn, you know how your Granddad is," cooed Grandmother, straightening up her clean plate. And with that, Satellite bounded out of the galley, brilliant emerald green bikini bouncing like a buoy.

Back in her room, Satellite drew her shades, then set her camera on the nightstand, plugging it into her laptop. Taking a look in the full-length mirror, she sighed with relief. Her spirit seemed to shine like some other-worldly star; the ocean had added a ravishing flourish that she really liked.

She gazed a while at her new turquoise tiger tooth necklace. Her fire red hair cascaded over the silver chain with a fierce vitality. Smiling, she moved to the bathroom, and slipping out of her emerald green bikini, popped into the shower. Cleansing herself with one of the many fragrant soaps that lined the fiberglass shell, Satellite stood covered in suds contemplating the day. Rinsing off, she grabbed a towel and dried her lithe physique. Wearing just a towel, she brushed her teeth in front of her bathroom sink. After finishing brushing, she hung her towel back up and donned her comfy pajamas.

Completely clean and refreshed, she prowled playfully over to her bed. She switched the lights off, and in the darkness, only the edge of her window was illuminated by the endless array of constellations outside. There, on the island of Kauai, along a stretch of remote wilderness, gently waving in the waters just offshore, aboard a ship named Lexeasure, up on the third deck, in her cozy quarters, nestled in the sheets of her bed, Satellite fell asleep.

Chapter 2
Meeting the Idens

The sun had just risen as Satellite sprang out of bed. Up and across the room, she flung open her closet revealing a kaleidoscope of colors, styles, patterns and prints. Tossing a floral sundress in the air, she fluidly pulled it over her head where it snugly fit her form.

"Satellite!" Grandmother called from the vaulted hallway outside her room, "Get yourself together, your Granddad is ready to go!"

"Almost ready!" Satellite called back as she dashed to the bathroom. Brushing her teeth, she excitedly fixed a sphinxlike look on her baby smooth face.

Hanalei was one of the most magical little towns in all of the Hawaiian Islands. Nestled at the foot of the mountains that lined the Na Pali Coast, there was an energy in the quaint shops there that stayed with people for a lifetime.

Dashing back out of the bathroom, she grabbed her backpack and swung it over her shoulder. Out into the vaulted hallway, down the stairs, and through the library and the lab to the galley. The aroma of coffee met her halfway along, and mouth watering, she nipped through the hatch of the galley to pick a breakfast treat from the kitchen.

Grandmother was inside sipping tea and looking out the window. "It's a beautiful day out there," she said. "And there's a bagel here with salmon spread, and there's coffee, tea, and milk and juice."

Staring out the window at the beauty of the island, Satellite picked up the salmon spread bagel and took a bite.

"Oh Hanalei, I do love that little town," Grandmother said with a nostalgic smile, "I hope you have a good day today, Satellite."

Finishing the salmon spread bagel and slurping down a glass of lilikoi juice, Satellite turned from the window to Grandmother. "I most certainly will; I've got some shopping I want to do," Satellite said, patting her backpack.

They shared a warm look over the drinks then Grandmother said, "Well, hurry along now, your Granddad is outside prepping the boat.

Satellite stepped in and hugged Grandmother. "Thank you, Grandmother." And with that, Satellite left the cozy embrace of Grandmother and the soft lights of the galley.

Backpack pulled high and tight on her young back, she strode through the Lexeasure to the tender garage. Granddad was already at the helm with the engine harumming steadily in the water.

"Climb aboard, Satellite," he said, looking over. "Let's get a move on."

Satellite climbed on aboard happily.

"All set?" he asked. "We've got a bit of a ride to Hanalei; luckily, it's the scenic tour the whole way." He beamed as he settled in and drove the boat out of the waterfilled tender garage.

"Vrummm!" sounded the engine as they accelerated. And then they were off, peeling out around the side of Lexeasure, out into open waters.

Zooming over the massive ocean swells, they made good

time. Rounding the rugged coastline that ran the length of a hiking trail for an unforgettable eleven miles, the first signs of civilization began to pop up. Families played on beaches lining the pure shores.

Racing onwards, they passed golden coves, rocky tide pools, tiny stores, and occasional neighborhoods. Sailing around a peninsula yielded a lovely view that seemed to be right out of a painting. Hanalei, nestled just by the bay and the mountains, felt like a home where the fireplace has burned itself down to the embers.

"I'll drop you off at the pier," Granddad said over the sound of the engine. "Then I've got some things to take care of. You have a good time now, and you have your phone so you can call me whenever you're ready." Granddad kissed Satellite on top of her head and pulled the boat around on the glassy water in front of the pier. "Off you go now, have fun!" Satellite climbed from the boat to the pier then turned around and waved.

"See ya!" she called as Granddad revved the boat and sped off.

Hoisting her backpack, Satellite made her way out and across the pier, looking up and to the right at the picturesque vision in front of her. The beach which she turned to walk on was pleasantly hushed, except for a scattered smattering of swimmers and people enjoying the morning.

She heard life stirring in the houses as she passed, like an orchestra warming up before it plays. Her flip flops were flicking shelly sand up on her toned calf muscles and the sensation felt great. Approaching a lifeguard tower, she waved a friendly good morning to a family setting up their accoutrements for a day at the beach. The family of five waved back, smiling, and wished her a good day.

Turning left at the lifeguard tower, Satellite entered the little road that led through the neighborhood to the energetic shopping center of Hanalei. A few homes later, where families could be heard clattering over a hearty breakfast or calling to each other from different rooms, Satellite came upon the first shop, Crystals and Gems Gallery.

Crystals and Gems Gallery was renowned for having exquisite artifacts, rare jewelry, and powerful earth minerals. Chimes sounded as Satellite pushed the door open, and a mystical rush of what seemed like all of Satellite's favorite feelings sourced over her.

The gallery was a tight cozy size, with curiosities covering every inch of free space. The shopkeeper looked up from cleaning some figurines and nodded warmly with bright eyes twinkling endlessly. Satellite lifted her chin and opened her hands, palms up as a response. The shopkeeper smiled with understanding and with a voice that sounded like it came from a night sky full of shooting stars said simply, "Welcome."

Satellite breathed in the fragrances of the shop and her eyes found a magnetic cube on display on the first shelf. Moving forward and looking around, she saw troves of pendants, talismans, crystals, minerals, statues, mini figurines, and totems, and as many magical oddities as the packed shop could contain.

Trembling a little with excitement, she picked up the magnetic cube. The cube was composed of many smaller cubes and could be rearranged as desired. Satellite loved treasures, and as she was at the premiere shop to acquire them, she rolled the cube around in her palm, then gripped it and moved along the shelf.

Large geodes caught her attention. They were a good energy, she felt, but a little big for her backpack. Moving along the shelf further, she discovered a collection of mini deity figurines and totems. Some were of angels; others were gods, with each holding weight.

Satellite saw the one she wanted, a chimera. Poised in a heroic stance, the chimera seemed to be gloriously in pursuit of some quest of passion and legend. Satellite picked up the chimera and held it up in her hand. She gasped silently, as she could feel the chimera, and she could feel the quest.

Her heart pounded for a few beats. Similar to her discovery of the turquoise tiger tooth, she sensed that this chimera totem was endowed with illumination. A little awe-struck, Satellite clutched the totem in her fist, the passionate pursuit of the chimera playing like a movie in her mind. Having discovered two treasures, Satellite looked reverently around for one more item to finish her purchase.

Opting for something crystalline, she moved past the assorted minerals to the crystal section. Nearly every geometric shape was represented in clear cut quartz, and seeing the spread of shapes in front of her, she let her fingers fly to the first one they flew to — the dodecahedron.

Satellite lifted it off the shelf, tossed it in the air, then swiped it into her hand. Three treasures, each unique, she beamed. Satellite purchased the items from the starry-voiced shopkeeper, then flung the door open and headed out into the island sunshine.

Backpack bouncing jauntily along with her in stride, Satellite crossed the main road and strode alongside the picnic tables that lined the sidewalk. As she walked, she looked left and right, taking in the quaint shops that stretched up and down the length of town.

An irresistible aroma met her and charmed her into a gentle frenzy of craving. It was the coffee shop, Hanalei Bread Company. "Oh my gosh," Satellite thought to herself, slumping her small shoulders forward and trudging with undeniable submission to the succulent calling of foods and drinks from within the coffee shop.

Up she went on the stairs, mouth watering, sniffing the scent of coffee richly brewed that hung like cumulonimbus clouds in the interior atmosphere. Bagels and pastries were crammed in the case along with muffins and cookies. With the place swimming in delights, Satellite looked up at the posted menu dizzy with anticipation.

"I would love to have one of the lattes with a chocolate croissant," Satellite told the barista with confidence.

"Absolutely, coming right up. Can I get a name with your order?" The barista inquired.

"It's Satellite," Satellite said.

"Satellite? Hey, aren't you the granddaughter of the couple who own Lilikoi Source and Omnikinetica?" the barista asked, looking over the treats that cluttered the counter.

"Yes, that's me," Satellite said, happy to hear that someone knew of her family so readily.

"For real?" exclaimed a handsome boy in a blue and white striped shirt standing next to her. "My family gets all our lilikoi juice from Lilikoi Source all the time." Reaching out his hand the boy said, "My name's Ionakana."

Satellite shook his hand in awe saying, "I'm Satellite."

"And this," Ionakana continued, gesturing to the countertop with sugar and cream where Satellite now noticed a small commotion was going on, "is my twin sister, Isla."

Satellite, who had been looking respectfully into Ionakana's sunbeam face, let out a giggle of mirth at the dancing melody that was Isla leggily swirling in sugar and splashing cream into her coffee before bouncing her booty over to Ionakana and Satellite.

"Hey, I overheard you guys; you're Satellite of Lilikoi Source. I'm Isla," she breathed excitedly. Satellite was best friends with Isla right then and there. Chattering insanely to each other, Satellite grabbed her drink, while Ionakana smiled and thanked the barista.

The group moved to a table, and with Isla and Satellite practically screaming with glee at each other, they all took a seat. Settling into their drinks and treats, Satellite told Ionakana and Isla, "You guys are the first I've talked to since moving out here to be with my grandparents."

Nipping at a croissant sandwich, Isla asked, "What is it that your parents do?"

Glancing proudly at the sky through the window for a moment, Satellite's gaze returned to Ionakana and Isla. "They're scientists. They were working at the CERN particle collider in Switzerland, but a classified job came up for them elsewhere in the world and that's why I'm with my grandparents now.

"Whoa! Classified! Nice!" exclaimed Ionakana and Isla together. "You lived in Switzerland?" Ionakana asked.

"Yes, for about seven years. It's a gorgeous country." Satellite replied with a soft sigh.

"Hey, I heard your grandparents live aboard a yacht. Is that true?" Isla asked sipping her drink. "Yes, the Lexeasure," Satellite answered, beaming.

"That's awesome," Ionakana whispered looking with

fascination at Satellite. Satellite nodded, munching into her chocolate croissant.

"Do your grandparents travel often, aboard the Lexeasure?" Isla asked.

"Yep, they're basically on a continuous cruise, but they do stay amongst the Hawaiian Islands for a lot of the time." Satellite said. "Granddad still stays busy with his tech company, Omnikinetica."

"Sounds like you're in a pretty much perfect position with both your parents and grandparents," Ionakana remarked, finishing his drink. "What about school, though?"

Satellite smiled. "Well, I finished high school in Switzerland," she said with satisfaction, "and now I'm thinking about what I want my future to be. What about you guys? What's your story?"

Ionakana and Isla looked at each other. "We've lived on Kauai here in Hanalei all our lives," Ionakana said, his voice carrying an exotic accent as he spoke. "This is where it's at for us."

The three of them pulsed quietly for a moment, eyes sparkling on the aromatic scene of the coffee shop around them.

"Well, listen, I have plans to go shopping for some new clothes, you guys want to join me?" Satellite asked reigniting the conversation.

"Sure!" Ionakana and Isla chimed together. "There's a store next door called Azure Island Clothing that I thought I'd check out and see if they have some articles for a new outfit I want to put together," Satellite said.

"We know the place, let's go," Ionakana and Isla had already started clearing the table.

And in a flourish of grace, the three teens cleaned the table, thanked the barista again, and gently ambled out of the cozy coffee atmosphere of Hanalei Bread Company.

Entering the sunshine filled walkway between the buildings, Satellite, Ionakana and Isla glanced around, waking from the happy trance they had drifted into.

"It's just over here," Ionakana called, pointing across the way at a small shop with its windows lined with colorful clothes in exotic prints. Making their way across the open space between the buildings, the three climbed the stairs to the shop front where a sign above the door read, "Azure Island Clothing".

The trio entered the sunlit shop and began to browse the garnished garments. Vibrant hues imbued the exotic plots of myriads of artistically articulated articles arranged amongst the ambience of the idea of the island scene motif.

Ionakana discovered a dashing drop-crotch jogger while Isla's fingers flew over a flamboyant blouse of floral blossoms. Satellite perused the pretty prints pausing only to pass pinnacle patterns across her positive perspective.

As Ionakana and Isla returned from the register with their new clothes, a jaunty juxtaposition jumped in front of them. Satellite stood smiling from ear to ear, her flaming red hair spilling over the shoulders of a plunging jungle print dress that rippled like water.

"Is this pop or what!" Satellite exclaimed. Ionakana and Isla laughed as Satellite purchased the dress, and the three new friends stepped out of the shop and back into the sunlight.

Strolling through the swarm of people amicably making their way up and down the sidewalk, the trio glanced with good natured looks in the eclectic shop windows as they passed. Satellite suddenly whipped around to see Ionakana and Isla. "Hey, I just had a thought. Would you guys like to cruise with my grandparents and me over to Oahu for a few days?"

Ionakana and Isla looked at each other excitedly. "We'd love to! Let me ask permission really quickly!" Ionakana said happily.

Stopping at a picnic table, Ionakana called their parents.

"My grandparents would love to entertain guests, and I've got some fantastic ideas for a cool YouTube video I'd love to make with you guys," Satellite said to Isla.

"We're good to go!" Ionakana said, gently gazing at Satellite. "We live pretty close, so my mom and dad are going to bring our packs to the pier."

They made their way down the quiet streets of Hanalei's neighborhood and reached the beach of the bay. Plodding across the shelly sand, they could see Granddad in the distance by the boat at the pier. As they reached the pier, Granddad looked up and waved. "You guys are just in time!"

"Granddad, is it OK if my new friends Ionakana and Isla come with us to Oahu this weekend?" Satellite asked.

"Sure, we've got more than plenty of room aboard," Granddad replied, smiling at Ionakana and Isla. Just then, Ionakana and Isla's parents pulled their car into the parking lot. They got out of the car and carried Ionakana and Isla's packs across the pier. Ionakana's father reached them and stuck out his hand for Granddad to shake.

"Icarus Iden, and this is my wife, Iris," Mr. Iden said as he shook Granddad's hand. "Heard a lot of about you folks, pleasure to meet you in person," Mr. Iden continued.

"Sol Sacavage, charmed to meet you. And this is my granddaughter, Satellite," Granddad chuffed happily.

The grownups talked while Satellite, Ionakana and Isla put the packs in the boat and climbed in. "I can't wait to show you guys the Lexeasure!" Satellite said excitedly.

"Ha! Yeah! This is awesome! Thanks, Satellite. And we've got our cameras and skateboards. We are good to go!" Isla said, beaming back.

"All right, all aboard!" Granddad said as he turned and stepped into the boat. The Idens waved goodbye as Granddad revved the engine, then pulled gracefully away from the pier and out into the open ocean.

The ride back along the Na Pali Coast was as beautiful as you can possibly imagine. Soaring mountains, sweeping beaches, and a sapphire shoreline flew past as the boat skimmed over the sea.

Sometime later, the Lexeasure came into view. Its stunning shape and fluid form produced a gorgeous gestalt that generated a plethora of ne plus ultra qualia, provoking lively futuristic concepts in all their mind's eyes.

Ionakana and Isla stared drop-jawed as they approached.

Granddad managed to maneuver the boat right into the side of the yacht's docking bay. A few of the usually unseen crew waited patiently to assist with docking and Granddad's supplies.

As they unloaded, Grandmother glided in. "Oh, guests! Welcome, welcome, and what are your names?"

"Ionakana and Isla Iden, pleased to meet you," said Ionakana, taking Grandmother's hand in his.

"Very nice to meet you. I hope you all are hungry; I've got finger sandwiches and fresh kombucha ready that we can take upstairs to the upper deck." They all gathered their things and followed Grandmother out of the garage's bay and into the

Lexeasure's labyrinth.

Moments later, they were all settled on the upper deck nipping on finger sandwiches and sipping kombucha.

"Now, we will be leaving for Oahu bright and early tomorrow morning, and your Granddad and I will be going out once we're there, so I hope you all are making plans," Grandmother said as she looked across the table at the trio.

"We're going to make a YouTube video. We've got our cameras, our skateboards, and a long list of locations to hit." Satellite said as she glanced to her left and to her right at Ionakana and Isla.

The simple lifestyle they shared sent a soothing silence around the table, as they all looked at Kalalau Beach simmering in the solar swath of the sanguine sunset.

Granddad cleared his throat as twilight overtook the ocean. "Satellite, why don't you show Ionakana and Isla to their rooms? We've got a busy day tomorrow, and you all need get a full nights' sleep to get your dreams in order."

And as the stars began to pop into the night sky, Satellite, Ionakana and Isla made their way off the upper deck and back into the elaborate labyrinth of the Lexeasure's interior. They climbed down a flight of stairs and cruised down the vaulted hallway to where Satellite's room was nestled next to the guest rooms.

Satellite stood outside her room and gestured at the guest rooms. Then with a loving look at Ionakana and Isla, she said, "I'm really glad I met you guys today. I find joy in solitude, but there is a palpable rapture in friendship, and you guys are just radiating with it." They all gleamed at each other, then they softly bid their goodnights and turned into their rooms.

Chapter 3
Coasting Along the Coast

As the heavens hoisted the sleepers' dreams over the heights of the horizon, dawn diffused the shimmering shoreline. The starchitecture of the superyachts' iconic pop rocked atop the cyan sea as the swash of waves serendipitously swathed the yacht in the sun's early morning rays.

Satellite's sparkling eyes opened in shining delight amidst the bliss of her bed and the lavish trappings of her rooms' bulkhead. She rose, well-rested, slipping her silken sheets into a straight line and cramming her comfortable comforter into the bed case.

She plumped her pillows, then pivoted into a springing caper over to the closet, where she slid into a baby blue bikini with a cream-colored romper over top. She then brushed her brilliantly white teeth, spritzed on some aromatic perfume, dashed a dazzling smile into her mirror, then strode across her room and opened the door to the vaulted hallway.

In the glossy gleam of the Lexeasure's lighting, Satellite rapped smartly on the doors to Ionakana and Isla's rooms. Their doors opened simultaneously. Isla was dressed to impress in an electro threaded color storm hooded dress and white high-top sneakers, with her long dark hair streaked with sun-blonded tousled skeins playfully cascading around her shoulders and chest.

Ionakana, on the other hand, had on black skinny jeans, a

black and white striped t-shirt, and red skate shoes with his thick brown and blonde hair swept to the side.

"I hope you guys are wearing your clothes over your swimsuits, because we are getting wet today!" Satellite said, keenly eying the siblings.

"Oh, that's an affirmative," Ionakana said, smiling.

"Yeah, we're Kauai kids, Satellite," Isla grinned. "We're always soaking."

Satellite laughed, "Right on! Well, let's head down to the galley and get some breakfast. We've got a big day ahead of us, and we gotta start it right."

The trio turned and marched off down the vaulted hallway to the yacht's staircase and made their way down. Strolling along through the beautiful rooms, they said good morning to a few crew members who were preparing for the morning's voyage.

As they opened the door and entered the galley, Granddad and Grandmother looked up from their tablets. "Well now, how is everyone on this very auspicious morning?" Granddad called over his coffee.

"Excited!"

"Doing well!"

"Really good!" said Satellite, Ionakana and Isla in turn.

"Scrambled eggs and sausage are on the table, and there's lilikoi juice, coffee and milk, just help yourselves," Grandmother said gently.

The three teens grabbed plates and drinks and seated themselves at the table.

"Now once we get to Oahu, your Granddad and I will be out and about, so you'll be on your own," Grandmother said.

Satellite looked up from scarfing down her eggs and

sausage. "We're going to go over to the salon after breakfast and plan out a hit list for all the spots we're going to go to for a YouTube video we're making."

Ionakana and Isla nodded fervently in agreement as Satellite continued. "We've got all of our cameras, a drone, and our skateboards."

"Very nice," Granddad said as he turned his head to look out the window. "It's a perfect day out there. I'd like to see the video after you edit it. I always like the music you choose."

Satellite, Ionakana and Isla finished eating, then cleaned their plates and put them in the dishwasher. As they each refilled their drinks, the Lexeasure revved its engines and began accelerating, causing the kids to almost spill their drinks.

"And we're off!" Granddad exclaimed. "I'm going to go check on the bridge," he said, as he got up from the table.

"We're off to the salon," Satellite called across the galley.

Grandmother only smiled as she gazed serenely out the window.

The salon was at the rear of the ship and was home to an astonishing array of very fashionable furniture. As the three friends entered holding their drinks, Satellite picked up a remote and clicked a button sending a television floating up through an entertainment center. "I like a little bit of background buzz," Satellite said idly as they all stretched out, carefree, on the clean conceptual couches.

As the trio talked, the jagged mountains of the Na Pali Coast and the shallow sea surrounding the cosmic Kalalau Beach were soon swallowed up by the ultramarine horizon.

"I'm thinking we head straight for Koko Marina and skate over to China Walls," Ionakana said pensively. "We can hit some flips, and then go jump Spitting Cave if you girls are up to it," he added, bobbing his head and making a baby face.

"I'm up for it!" Satellite said innocently.

"Yeah, that'll be a bomb warm up," Isla said glancing a gentle glare at Ionakana; but she couldn't contain herself and broke into a smile.

Ionakana swigged his drink, "What about Hawaii Kai skate park next? We can get some lines, get some grinds, have a good time, then pop over to Sandy's Beach and get barreled."

Satellite and Isla stirred in stimulation, their perky physiques piqued. "Game," Satellite said solidly. "It'll be evening after the beach, we'll probably wanna grab a bite to eat. But you know what I really want to do? I dance. Do you guys know of any good clubs?"

"Ohhh!" shouted Ionakana and Isla together, raising their arms rollercoaster style in unison. "Starnectar! It's the sickest venue in Honolulu, and there's always a big-name DJ playing!" Isla exclaimed excitedly.

"Yeah, we gotta go there, you have to see it!" Ionakana said, clutching his ceramic coffee cup, his eyes flashing with youthful fire. "It's super futuristic; all modded out top to bottom with lasers everywhere."

"Hmmm," Satellite mused with a mirthful look on her amused face. "Well gee, lemme think here… OK!" She squealed with a cheeky wink.

"It's set then", Ionakana noted to the girls. "We've got day one squared away. I'd say a trip to the North Shore would be a good way to follow up to all that. We can hit Waimea Bay and get the jump rock, then cruise over to Shark's Cove for snorkeling. After that I'd say a little session at the Banzai Skatepark, then hop across the street and catch the sunset at

Pipeline Beach."

"North Shore, good to go. But let's not plan too far ahead. We might get other ideas as the day goes on," Isla remarked sagely.

"We've got two excellent days in the works," Satellite added. "Let's set our schedule to a simmer for now. I like open space for spontaneity."

Ionakana nodded in agreement while Isla puckered her lips at the ocean view out the window.

Satellite, Ionakana and Isla passed the time swapping stories while the movie '20,000 Leagues Under the Sea' played in the background.

After a while, Satellite stood up. "You guys wanna go up to the bow and look over the ocean towards Oahu? We should be getting close."

The trio slid off the clean conceptual couches and sauntered out of the salon and into galley. They made their way up the Lexeasure at a leisurely pace. They passed through the galley, Granddad's lab, and the library. All the while, Satellite pointed out the bright coastal paintings that lined the shiny white walls.

They ascended the superyacht's staircase and walked up the vaulted hallway to the hatch that opened up to the bow. A beautiful breeze greeted them cheerily as they opened the hatch and stepped out onto the front deck.

The rolling cobalt ocean churned endlessly in all directions under cotton-like clouds as the island of Oahu grew larger in the distance ahead of them.

"Ahoy down there!"

Turning to look up at the bridge two decks above, Satellite, Ionakana and Isla waved at Granddad, who was leaning against the railing.

"Got everything planned out?" Granddad called.

"For the most part!" Satellite called back. Granddad nodded, smiling, and returned his gaze to the sight of the island on the horizon.

Satellite, Ionakana and Isla stayed on the sunny bow talking animatedly for the remainder of the morning voyage. They couldn't have asked for better weather, Satellite thought, as the Lexeasure pulled into a mooring just offshore of Waikiki. Satellite, Ionakana and Isla surveyed the bustling beach and sunlit streets teeming with people on shopping sprees under the distinct skyline, with Diamond Head Crater just off to the side by the sea.

"Grab your packs, we're going ashore!" Granddad called from above them on the bridge. Turning from the beautiful view in front of them, the trio headed back through the hatch, down the vaulted hallway into their rooms, grabbed their packs and skateboards, then made their way downstairs to the tender garage where the shore boat would take them into town.

They entered the tender garage moments later where Granddad and Grandmother stood dressed in beach clothes with a member of the crew who was already behind the wheel. Grandmother simply beamed at them while Granddad nodded at their packs then winked a twinkling blue eye. "All aboard!" he said, smiling.

The three friends clambered eagerly into the boat and settled into their seats. The grandparents followed, climbing in easily, and sat comfortably in the seats just behind the driver.

The driver peeled the boat out from the tender garage of the Lexeasure, then revved the engine gently, and purred the little vessel atop the periwinkle waters to the crowded coastline.

The boat ride was but a mere minute.

Swimmers of all races were laughing and screaming in the sun-soaked shallows of the swelling shore as Satellite and the squad hopped from the boat to their quads where the sea meets the white sand of the busy beach.

Satellite stared eastward at the sky and the beach, then turned to face everybody. "We're heading to Hawaii Kai, but we'll be back in Waikiki by nightfall," Satellite promised the grandparents.

"We'll be with friends; just call and check in if you need to, and you have the number to get the crew to pick you up and take you back to the Lexeasure," Granddad said as he slid on a pair of sunglasses and flashed his famous grin.

"And be safe now, the camera is the biggest instigator of injuries there is," Grandmother said as she hoisted her beach tote to her shoulder and slipped her arm through Granddad's.

Satellite, Ionakana and Isla began picking their way up the beach towards the bus stop while Granddad and Grandmother set off in the opposite direction.

The bus ride was an absolute blast. Satellite and the siblings talked serenely as they gazed out the bumbling bus's windows at the beautiful island views. They rounded out of Waikiki and made their way through the eclectic Kaimuki community, then passed Kahala Mall.

Continuing eastward, it was while they were zooming through Aina Haina when Isla excitedly interjected. "Guys, there is a gorgeous path that winds through the back of Aina Haina valley and leads up to the top of the Ko'olau Mountain spine. Just know that it's incredible, and if you ever get a chance to hike it, do it." Ionakana and Satellite nodded, their eyes filling with lush jungle wonder.

The bus made its way down Kalaniana'ole Highway, passing Niu Valley then crossing over a bridge to where the sky opened up around them and Hawaii Kai stretched out before them.

They crossed another bridge at the bay, then rumbled down the road just a little further to where the bus made a left-hand turn.

"This is us!" Ionakana exclaimed. The trio thanked the bus driver then stepped out onto the sidewalk. As the bus motored on its way, the three friends turned and looked across the clean street.

"Koko Marina. One of the greatest little places on the island," Ionakana said stoically.

"Well, let's check it out then," Satellite said eagerly, "And maybe grab a bite to eat too." They darted across the street in the shade of the trees that lined the median, went down a staircase, crossed a parking lot, and then found themselves in a practically perfect plaza.

"Well, this sure is a super little square we've got here!" Satellite exclaimed stoutly.

The trio glanced amicably from the movie theater on their right to the bobbing boats across the way in the marina. "We're burning precious daylight. Let's grab a mochi bite from Bubbies Ice Cream, then head over to China Walls," Isla said gently gesturing to the ice cream parlor ahead of them.

Satellite, Ionakana and Isla quickly queued up in the quirky parlor of Bubbies, bought some mochi bites, then flung open the door and quixotically continued their charming quest to China Walls.

They passed the cute shop fronts while nibbling on their

mochi bites.

Finishing off the last bit of his guava mochi, Ionakana looked skyward and said, "Isla is right. We're burning daylight; let's hop on our boards and skate through Portlock to the Walls."

The girls nipped down the rest of their mochi then tossed their boards down and kicked off. The three friends had a blast as they boosted through the beautiful neighborhood of Portlock. Popping off the sidewalks, they swooped, carved, shredded and ripped their way up and down the concrete streets, getting classy camera footage as they went.

They pulled up half an hour later sweaty and looking sun-flushed to the cul-de-sac in front of China Walls.

"Chee-hoo! All right, let's flippin' huck some into the ocean!" Ionakana yelled. Satellite and Isla scooped up their skateboards then shook their shiny hair in the sun and sprayed a squealing scream skywards as they sprinted to the sea.

Stripping down seconds later into their swimsuits, the young squad unsheathed their cameras and the drone, then stood steadfast and primed at the jump spot. The cerulean sea shone before them from atop the famous twenty-foot-tall rock ledge of China Walls that encircled the southeast section of Portlock.

Setting her bare feet in a gymnast's starting position, Satellite fired off the friends' flipping frenzy with a flawlessly formulated double front flip.

"That was perfect!" the siblings shouted as Satellite swam up through the surface moments later. As Satellite climbed out, she glanced over the shoulder of her beautiful bikini clad body just in time to see Ionakana huck a burly gainer to can opener ocean entrance.

"First try no warmup!" Ionakana belted out as he muscled through the water easily and grabbed hold of the rock wall.

As Satellite and Ionakana rejoined Isla at the jump spot, Isla handed over the camera to Satellite. "OK, front flip to dive coming right up!"

True to her word, Isla executed a perfect one and half making the tiniest splash of a splash humanly possible. Isla bobbed up buoyantly and took a breath with her bodacious face as she basked unabashed in flabbergasted laughter at the spectacular feat she had just tackled.

As the sun slowly circled in the sky, the squad savagely sent spinning somersaults into the surging summer swell. After about an hour, and oodles of uber couth youthful flipping footage later, the gang propped their legs up on the rock wall and peacefully panted in the picturesque panorama, where the prismatic arc of a ravishing rainbow had just revealed itself.

"All right, you girls," Ionakana said, smiling. "I think I can safely say that we worked this spot for about all it's worth."

The three friends chuckled as they looked at China Walls, then took a step back and stood proudly admiring each other's bodies.

"Well, I wanna jump Spitting Cave," Satellite said earnestly. "Yeah, me too," Isla responded with resounding soundness.

"All right," Ionakana said grinning, "Grab your packs, it's just around this rock-walled section of the coast here."

The three teens grabbed their gear, then streamed off with a lively stride. After a short meandering jaunt along the rock wall, Satellite, Ionakana and Isla stood atop the perilous precipice of Spitting Cave.

Spitting Cave was an ocean cliff of nearly sixty feet with a huge cave of doom at the bottom. With every wave that surged forward into it, it rebounded it and forced a sizable spit back out.

"I can go first to show you how it's done," Ionakana said aside to Satellite, who stood beside him.

Satellite said nothing as she shouldered past and strode to the launch rock. Quickly whipping the camera out of his pack, Ionakana hastily hurried after Satellite, Isla following suit.

In one fluid motion, Satellite stepped to the enormous edge, shook back her mane of ruby red hair with its sun-bleached tips, then sprung up and out bringing her chin back and straightening her body as she swept backwards in an absolutely ginormous gainer.

The moment was other-worldly. A slow rotation, suspended in a seemingly leisurely levitation, then the wind roared and reality re-materialized as Satellite ecstatically shot out a primal shriek of pristine energy that reverberated in raw purity against the cliff as she hit the blue abyss.

Ionakana and Isla stood silently stunned staring down the steep relief of Spitting Cave to where Satellite was still submerged in the sea.

"Fwaaah!" Satellite ecstatically gasped as her bubbling face breached the foam in front of the cave.

"That was incredible!" Ionakana shouted down while still holding the camera up.

"You gotta swim out before the swell sucks you into the cave!" Isla yelled down.

Easy as the breeze, Satellite smiled up at the siblings, then swam over to the reefy rock ledge and climbed out of the ocean. A moment later, Satellite had climbed the cliff and rejoined Ionakana and Isla at the top.

"That was an amazing first time for Spitting Cave, Satellite; most people just jump it, you know," Ionakana said, smirking. "That gainer though... seemed like it was spiritual..." Ionakana trailed off as his eyes moved with impressed respect over Satellite's gleaming body.

"Well shoots, I'm just going to jump it," Isla said, still gazing at Satellite in astonishment.

"Right, yeah, let me get a front flip real quick. Then I say we make our way over to the skate park," Ionakana said, recollecting himself.

With her shoulders back and a huge sparkle in her eye, Satellite took the camera and captured Isla's joyful jump, followed by a graceful flung-out diving front flip from Ionakana.

After the siblings had climbed the cliff and rejoined Satellite at the top, they all grabbed their packs and threw backwards glances at the great galvanizing jump of Spitting Cave.

Chapter 4
Swashbuckle at Starnectar

After a brisk barge through Portlock on their boards and a brief bus ride later, the trio rolled up to the Hawaii Kai Skate Park. The skate park was a giant square complete with bowls, ledges, a flat bar rail, hips, a euro gap, pockets and a pyramid.

As they entered, the local boys all threw shakas and smiled at them with glowing aloha. Satellite, Ionakana and Isla walked up a slope and put their packs down on a low curving ledge.

"Listen, I'm a bit of a ripper," Ionakana said eying the park. "And if you don't mind, I'm going to get a line so fine, drop a heavy grind, slow down time then flick a trick so smooth, you know, the automatic kind." Ionakana had a very sharkish smile solidly spread across his tropical teenage face as Satellite and Isla grinned appreciatively at his poetic words.

"Cool, I'll film," Satellite said grabbing the camera out of her pack.

After about a dozen tries, Ionakana got the line. With a running start, he charged along the backside of the park where he then popped into a deep smith grind on the tall curved ledge pocket. He popped out then pushed twice before he sprang up and clanged into a perfect bangarang backside 50-50 grind on the flat bar rail. After landing, he raced through the corner where their packs were, then busted a huge ollie and cleared the large slope they had walked up. Stomping the ollie clean at the bottom of the slope, he got another few pushes in, then boosted up the pocket quarter pipe in the corner, coming down fakie, where he proceeded to let loose a beautiful full cab flip on the hip.

Raising his hands in triumph, Ionakana got a standing ovation from the local boys and Isla. Satellite, who had been following with the camera, cruised over and gave Ionakana a happy hug. The trio then took turns filming as they skated the different obstacles.

Satellite and Isla decided on a chill session and kept to the bowls, where they locked into all kinds of grinds and stalls on the coping while pumping through the transitions and launching airs into the afternoon atmosphere.

After getting a satisfactory amount of good skate footage, Satellite, Ionakana and Isla returned to their packs in the corner, sweaty and sore.

"If we catch the next bus, we can fit in some body surfing at Sandy Beach," Isla said checking her phone.

"Yeah, we gotta hurry. I'd like to catch some waves just as sunset hits," Ionakana said hoisting his pack.

"Ooh! I've been looking forward to Sandy's," Satellite said smiling.

As they headed out of the park and across the grass to the bus stop, one of the young local boys in the park shouted out a lively, "Shoots!" after them. Their eyes flashed appreciatively as they exchanged knowing looks. Just as they got to the bus stop, the bus ambled on over, right on time.

A short while later, they were trotting across Sandy Beach Park, eyes full of intrigue as they scoped out the crushing shore break tubes. Sandy Beach Park, or just Sandy's as it was commonly called, was the stomping grounds for some of the best bodysurfers in the Hawaiian Islands. The waves here swelled up to massive size and broke in very shallow water, creating thrilling barrel rides and dangerous over-the-falls conditions. As Satellite, Ionakana and Isla took a seat in the sand, they looked around as they retrieved their cameras.

All the "Who's Who of Oahu" were at Sandy's with photo framed faces and friends with formidable form. A number of videographers were positioned both on the beach and in the tube slots for barrel shots.

"All right Satellite, Sandy's can make or break you," Ionakana said seriously. "Get your barrel and charge through it, and try not to get pulled over the top. These are big waves with occasional freak breakers that are even bigger. Oh, and bee tee dubs, everyone here is watching."

Satellite and Isla acknowledged Ionakana's warning and resolutely got to their feet. "I just hope my bikini doesn't get ripped off and I gotta search for it in the nude in front of all these burly boys," Satellite said with a twinkle in her eye and a blush on her cheeks.

Isla chuckled as she brushed the sand off her bottom and calmly looked out over the roiling whitewash and clear waves. Ionakana chortled as he clambered on up then looked at the sea smiling. "Well... apart from the risk of washing up on the beach completely naked in front of all these people and cameras, I think we'll be able to snag some sexy shacks with our suits on, sound good?"

"Sounds good!" Satellite and Isla sang out in unison. At that, they all sprinted off over the sand and dove into the dreamy dollops of whirling whitewash.

Once in the ocean, the scene was that of a serene clean intermittent with the swoop of salty cylinders, where bodysurfers leaned into rip-roaring reams as cameras clicked and rolled and the beach bound crowd, when pleased, cheered and teased as the sun sank lower and the breeze tousled the pretty palm trees.

Satellite waded in the warm, glassy, robin's egg blue waters, allowing the sifting sand to tickle her toes as the setting sun softly seared its solar kiss onto her smooth skin, sending her into the dear depths of existential bliss. Just then, a big watery wedge came reeling out of the blue.

"That's you!" Isla squealed from behind Satellite. "Camera's rolling!" Ionakana shouted from next to Isla.

Pushing off from the bottom, Satellite paddled fiercely in front of the wave, where she then felt herself drawn into the forceful flume. Flinging out her forearm, she fluidly flew over the face of the wave and swooped into the barreling blue tube. Like a moment frozen in time, Satellite stared through the barrel's beam that was lit from the rolling throw like a crystalline chandelier. Ionakana's curious countenance cruised through the watery wall as Satellite sped past his camera that was capturing the action. As the barreling wave carrying Satellite surged into the seashore's shallows, it swelled over itself and sent Satellite spiraling over the falls and into the whimsical fit of the whitewash.

Just as Satellite surfaced, she caught sight of Isla's wet hair whipping in the wind as her bombshell body was whisked through the tube of a rapidly wrapping whitecap.

Satellite barely had time to congratulate Isla before Ionakana had flexed his way into a raging breaker, camera in hand, smile on his face, and a sparkle in his eye. As he blasted down the barrel, he swiveled a succinct three-sixty as he screeched out a child-like, "Chee-hoo!" and cannon-balled over the capsizing crest.

As the teenage trio teamed back together, they laughed aloud in the shallows where the tide's tumultuous turbulence tossed and turned in twilight's technicolor testament to the thriving therapeutic twinkling of the timeless stars. A frenzied feeling of freedom had enveloped the friends, and as the Earth turned and the night sky soared overhead, they rapturously romped like rabid raptors in the revealing of the sea's reality to their imagination's realizations.

Panting, with the stars pin-pointed like particles in their pupils, they picked up their packs and plodded across the pristine beach scene to rinse off with the loud crowd at the showers. After carefully cleansing their corporeal forms in the crystal-clear cascade from the conduit, Satellite turned to the chiseled silhouettes of Ionakana and Isla.

"There's only one way to finish off a day like today. I say we hit that club you mentioned and get a dance in."

"Oh, Starnectar! Oh my gosh, Satellite, wait until you see this place; it is something else!" Ionakana sang out in praise as Isla bobbed her head excitedly.

It was with butterflies in their bodies that the three teens set off on the bumbling bus with the other beachgoers back to the bustling block party of Waikiki.

One bus ride later, and they were popping off the bus into the pleasantly populated playground pulsing with rich kids, club hopping in the pretty lights of Waikiki's night life. Just up ahead of them, a large well-lit sign read, "Starnectar," in very crisp cursive script. Eyes wide with delight, Satellite, Ionakana and Isla exchanged bright smiles.

"Well, let's get our booties in there," Satellite said smartly.

They then primly strode up to the club and ascended the

stairs, passing the red velvet ropes in single file, Satellite in the lead. The bouncer at the door asked Satellite their age and when she replied, "Eighteen," he affixed a bracelet to each of their wrists that said in print, "No Alcohol". Shrugging unconcernedly, they pushed back a curtain and stepped forward.

The scene that greeted them was so verily vivacious it seemed to have come straight from the silver screen. Lasers jetted jagged patterns as they sizzled the airwaves in synch with the soulful synthesized sounds that salubriously seared their ears. The dapperly decorated den was packed to the brim with a beautiful boutique of uniquely lovable clubbers bouncing to the bountiful beat.

"Whoa!" Ionakana exclaimed, staring straight over the top of the sharking scenesters at the super-illuminated stage. "That's JettySet! He's a local Hawaiian DJ that's toured the club scene internationally!"

"Oh wow!" Isla said, surprised. "What are the chances we'd run into him! He's got albums out!"

"I like those songs he did like, 'Turquoise', 'Scrawny Boy', and 'Star-Struck Silhouette'," Isla chimed as her dazzled face drank in the superstar DJ.

"Geez, I've never seen him before. He's really got that Versace look, doesn't he?" Satellite said as she raked him with an appraising eye.

Just then, JettySet looked over from the ferocious festival at his fingertips and locked eyes with Satellite. His jaw dropped a little and his gaze gave her a slow once over. Both wearing eager expressions of awe-struck attentiveness, Satellite and JettySet shared an exclusive emphatic stare amidst the charming chaos of the carefree club.

"Wow, why don't you two get a room, you're practically making out in here," Isla said breathlessly to Satellite while holding in a gentle giggle.

JettySet flashed a dashing smile, then directed his focus back to his set with a flourish. Satellite's heart was racing rapidly as her bosom ballooned ever so slightly in and out.

That look... Satellite thought to herself. That look had pounded a palpable peacefulness into the prettiest pieces of her nubile mind.

"Uh, Earth to Satellite," Ionakana said bringing her back to the moment. Satellite let loose a low whistle then tossed back her ruby red hair.

Revved up from their rambunctious day, Satellite, Ionakana and Isla exchanged rowdy eyebrows, then gaily roll-stepped forward into the rave's fray. Dancing deftly with the dramatic deliriousness of a daft dream, the three teens mobbed the middle of the dance floor like the most posh mosh pit ever seen.

The lasers, the lights, the smiles, the eyes, the way the music ignited every neuron of her mind. Satellite, feeling such a perfect paradisiacal prerogative to preen, shot JettySet's shiekish physique a sultry stare with her flawless face fixed in its sphinx-like vision that she held to so vehemently with her visceral volition.

Suddenly, through the throbbing throng, Satellite lithely leapt onto the illuminated stage and smartly secured JettySet's microphone in her manicured hand. Over the top of JettySet's lush electro track, Satellite sang forth a song so saturated in serendipitous beauty that the entire club stood agape with awe at the sound of her spectacular spiritual strength that stood upon the stage like an obelisk of vox. As the song reached a node in its nexus, Satellite nodded and switched modes into a full on free-flowing show, sending the whole club into a state of fresh effervescence and glow in excelsis.

Satellite was mixing an extremely expressive elixir of vigorous vocals with the heavy hitting boisterous beat of the tropical track, when she noticed she had JettySet's avidly aware attention upon her. He was boyishly bouncing and bobbing his head, drinking in her delightful depiction of his dressy electronic set. As their eyes met again, she saw his gorgeous gaze dart with absolute astonishment to the turquoise tiger tooth she still had embellishing her neck.

Satellite winked and waved the mic, returning to her groove as she waxed poetic to the way the tune moved the mood of all those in the room. As JettySet wrapped the track, the song Satellite was singing to was brought into a tasteful transition with the next auditory addition to the evening.

Satellite, seeing Ionakana and Isla smiling from ear to ear, raised the mic aloft to thunderous applause and cheers. As Satellite handed the mic back to JettySet, he set his set on automatic and addressed the club with his best. "Ladies and gentlemen, boys and girls, clubbers, scenesters and ravers, we have just been blessed tonight with an angelic voice that has transported our minds to the beautiful realms of this pretty young thing's ethereal existence."

JettySet now turned to face Satellite. "By the way, what is your name?"

Satellite turned to face JettySet. "Satellite, Satellite Sacavage."

JettySet smiled sagely. "Florian, Florian Faleafine. AKA JettySet."

Serenely sizing her up with a simmering stare, he

continued. "Listen, you have an otherworldly voice, and while you were singing, I had a fantastic foresight of featuring you on a new pop banger I've got in the works." With a wink, his eyes alighted again upon the turquoise tiger tooth on Satellite's chest. "Also, you've been in the valley beyond Kalalau Beach, because I gifted that necklace to the maze in the heart of the jungle not long ago."

Satellite stared, star-struck, at JettySet's fine face, her third eye swimming in the vision of the place in space she had gleaned from the gleam of the turquoise tiger tooth necklace.

"Tell you what, come to my house, 772 Ahuwale Street tomorrow morning bright and early. I've got a full recording studio where we can mash out a smash hit, no problem. And you're more than welcome to bring your friends too; they can make some backing vocals for the track."

The ambience of Satellite's aura was azure as she stood sure-footed and stretched out her arm to shake JettySet's hand. An alluring arc of energy sparked a syzygy between the two as JettySet took her hand in his and shook it savvily. Satellite's heart was happy as she heartily hopped off the stage where JettySet was now returning to his hosting of the smooth couth highbrow hullabaloo.

"And in one fell swoop, the sword was wrenched from the stone!" Isla exclaimed as she jumped forward and gave Satellite a congratulatory hug. "Satellite, you just morphed into a miracle and mesmerized the whole club up there! And now you've got one of the biggest beatmakers in the islands hounding after your sound!" Ionakana said in a flabbergasted floundering state as he flung back his fleek hair.

Satellite merely beamed as the siblings amicably appraised her eye-opening deed that was still emanating from her seamlessly.

"Well, we've got an early morning and a big day ahead of us tomorrow, so I say we head back to the Lexeasure for the night," Satellite said to the siblings.

The siblings nodded and the teen team strode through the club with a newfound sheen making a pickup call to the Lexeasure's crew as they exited Starnectar's scene, their sweat steaming in the clean breeze of Waikiki.

After a winding walk and a brief boat ride, Satellite, Ionakana and Isla stepped back aboard the iconic yacht. The trio trekked through the tender garage then trooped through the adjoining rooms before swooping into the galley for something smooth to drink and a late-night bite to eat. Satellite, followed by Ionakana and Isla, pushed open the door and discovered Granddad and Grandmother at the table laughing and relaxing while sipping champagne in their silken sleepwear.

"Good day?" Granddad said simply with a soft look.

"We had wings on our feet, the sun on our shoulders, the horizon in our eyes, and each other's greatness in our faces," Satellite said sanguinely.

Granddad sipped slowly at his champagne, savoring the wonderful bubbles as he let out a low guttural rumble with no trouble that rose from his muscled stomach.

"We stopped at the Starnectar Club, and Satellite sang like an angel in front of everyone!" Isla blurted out. "And now she's got a session in the morning to sing on a JettySet song!"

Grandmother stirred and turned in her chair. "Sounds like some boy heard how scrumptious my little Satellite is and wants to scooch in a bit," she said with a protective purr.

"Well, that may be so," Satellite said slowly with a sly

smile, "But I am genuinely thankful for the opportunity. We could make a song that gets radio play or even something he puts on for live shows," she edged on earnestly.

"Well, you two keep an eye on them," Grandmother said to Ionakana and Isla. "Try to keep it professional," she added with a blinked wink.

"Now, we're going to be entertaining guests aboard all day tomorrow," Grandmother continued. "You mentioned that you all were going to cruise through the North Shore. Will you have time after you work on your song?"

"I think so," Satellite replied, "We'll see how things go." "Just be safe in all you do," Grandmother said as she gracefully finished the last skosh of champagne then placed the empty glass on the table. The grandparents warmly swapped a watchful look then rose restfully from the table. "We're off to bed," Grandmother said, "You all have fun tomorrow. And Satellite, you give that boy one thrill of a trill to fill his sill." And with that, the grandparents left the galley for the night.

Sharing a misty-eyed look full of the vision of their mission, the three friends quickly picked their way through the fridge in the galley's kitchen for a smidgen of something to nip into. After grabbing their snacks and some lilikoi juice, Isla turned to Satellite with a toothy flash and a laugh that blasted the whole room.

"What a great day!" she exhaled. "We jumped, flipped, dove, hit the cliffs, skated, rode and shot through those waves so crisp! And then Starnectar! Satellite, what are you going to sing about tomorrow on JettySet's song?"

Satellite's eyes searched the skies through the stellar surface of the ceiling's rise. "Something along the lines of how

57

it took eons for our spirits to arise on this beautiful jewel we call Earth. Mix that with everything that makes me clean and happy and gives purpose and meaning to this world. And it wouldn't hurt to make it cute booty music too," Satellite said with a bubble in her virtuous voice that was in tune with the music of their fortuitous day.

Ionakana and Isla exchanged elated expressions. "Well, you've got the chops of a cherub," Ionakana said seriously, "And honestly, I think you're about to unleash a beast of a dream into the hearts and minds of a teeming sea of people."

Satellite nodded, a sense of duty deluging her until she was practically drenched and dripping with daring determination to divulge her dearest desires.

"I've got to get to that song," Satellite said, in the same sonic signature as the song she had sung at Starnectar.

At that, the trio tidied up the galley, strolled up the ship, stepped up the staircase, veered around and down the vaulted hallway, and whisked into their respective rooms with a whispered valediction.

After cleaning up for the night and dressing down, Satellite tucked into her pristine sheets and pulled them up to her pretty little dimpled chin. In the privacy of her personal space, Satellite plucked the turquoise tiger tooth from under the collar of her pajama top and held it placidly in her palm. As she gently drifted off to sleep, the fantastic phantasmagoria of the day played out under her eyelids, mixed with hints of friendly figures in formation that seemed to snap to attention in time with the lulling rhythm of the Lexeasure's oceanic habitation.

Chapter 5
Smile of My Mind's Eye

A knock, knock, knock sounded as Satellite rapped on the door to 772 Ahuwale Street. The sun had just risen and was shining its light over the quiet island and splaying some rays into the now-stirring neighborhood of Aina Haina Valley. Ionakana and Isla stood just behind and to either side of Satellite in her prime waiting in the sunrise for JettySet to arrive.

JettySet's home was a quaint Hawaiian style house on the hill with a turquoise roof and a well-kept fenced yard. Footsteps padded towards them from the interior of the house, and upon their arrival at the door, it swung open to reveal JettySet standing with vigor, dressed fashionably in a head-to-toe technicolor baroque matching outfit.

"Aloha!" JettySet said, dashing a smashing smile. "Come in, come in! The session is ready!"

Satellite peered around the well-lived-in living room that had a beautiful view of the ocean blue through the windows two. The trio kicked off their shoes in the vestibule, then looked at JettySet's chipper countenance for what to do.

After a clap of his handsome hands, JettySet gestured over his shoulder. "I've got one of the guest rooms situated as a studio. I say we dive right in and write some lines for starters. I've got a whole trove of tracks to throw down for your lyrical path," JettySet said as he turned and led Satellite and the siblings around the living room, down a short hall, and into a futuristic room that was the studio booth.

The siblings scooted through the tech-riddled room and assumed their seats in some chairs on wheels that were free to move. Satellite squared up to JettySet and swung her pack off her back, gladly extracting a notepad. "I woke up in the night and stayed up scratching out the tibs and tabs of my happy plans and am still thinking of the song name as best I can," Satellite said. "Here are the lyrics," she continued, handing JettySet the notepad. "But I think it should be called, 'Smile of My Mind's Eye'."

The siblings sparkled silently for a second then broke into a buzz. JettySet squinted in a suave, cosmopolitan sort of way, then searched the lyrics to see if they were up to par with the bar he had set for songs in the raw to garner radio play.

After keeping Satellite on tenterhooks for the time it took for him to take in the tantalizing task behind the truth in her titillating lyrical movements, JettySet turned the notepad over and returned it to her with a learned flick of the wrist, and where a burning look was the gist on his yearning face's bliss.

"Sing it," JettySet said simply.

Satellite coruscated. JettySet seated himself at his system and pointed to the glistening metallic microphone, already activated and listening. In the soft brightness of the sunrise streaming through the skylight, Satellite seemed to step through a portal and transform into an oracle, with her voice pouring forth as if her vocal cords were torquing choice noises from other worlds.

With the cosmos channeling through the sleek and cheeky celestial character that was her fair raspberry haired avatar, Satellite, once again, sang of a plane of existence that contained all the heavenly imaginings of a deity brain. JettySet sat in rapture, relishing the rejuvenating tune of Satellite's spirit serenading the soundproofed.

As Satellite finished the song with a cinch, she glanced at JettySet and the siblings to find their visions filled with the crystal-clear creation that her maiden presentation of "Smile of My Mind's Eye" had so earnestly endeavored to instill with its intrinsic inclination.

Starry-eyed and drop-jawed, JettySet saved the song on his system.

"Satellite, I think we may have just captured some real magic with that," JettySet said. "In one take, too," he continued, obviously awestruck. "Ionakana, Isla, let me get you two on the mic now for some backing vocals that I'll modulate later into synthesized sounds for some added sensation."

As the siblings belted out some backing vocals for the track, Satellite seated herself next to JettySet. "Hey, thanks for inviting us over. We really love your music, and I hope this gives you a kind of diamond in the rough to work on." Satellite said sincerely.

"Oh, no worries! I think once I get this song fully equipped with all the exotic pitches and riffs of island style music, it could be an international hit," JettySet said as he sat rapt, regarding her with a truly holistic fascination.

Satellite leaned in a little and pressed a question that she wanted answered. "This turquoise tiger tooth necklace… what's it's story?"

JettySet stared straight ahead for a second then said, "In due time, I'll tell you."

A short while later, the siblings had wrapped up their off-the-cuff and robust rough cut of track-backing vocals with love.

"OK, you guys," JettySet said, clicking his system, "I've got what I need to have to work on. This is where I dig in for the win," He smiled. "You guys are welcome to hang out…" he trailed off, looking at the trio.

"Oh awesome, thank you!" Satellite said happily. "But we've got plans to roar through the North Shore!"

JettySet laughed, flashing a glacier white set of teeth. "Sounds good! I'll let you know when the song is set in stone!"

At that, Satellite, Ionakana and Isla grabbed their packs, bounded out of the house, and resumed their pleasurable path that they just had to have.

A wild while later, the three teens had travelled by rumbling bus through the historic Hale'iwa town on their way to a great day on the North Shore, all the while waiting on updates from JettySet as he made leeway on "Smile of My Mind's Eye".

"I really hope that one take was as suitable for the song as JettySet said so," Satellite mused as they made their way off the bus at Waimea Bay.

"Satellite, you straight up killed it!" Isla said gently exasperated. "We all nearly went blind seeing how bright that smile in your mind's eye shines!"

Reassured and relaxed, Satellite, Ionakana and Isla passed some bubbly barefoot beachgoers babbling as they stepped onto the expansive sandy beach, complete with a jump rock that looked to be about twenty feet tall. The trio threw down their towels on the renowned ground and sat cross-legged as they simmered on the shore of the beautiful bay with the surrounding shimmering town.

"So, how about that spark between you and JettySet?" Isla

postulated to Satellite with playful pompousness.

"Well, I'm not going to lie, he is one freakishly fine fox," Satellite said tossing back her scarlet locks and squinting out at the sea.

Ionakana gazed at Satellite for a second, then spoke. "You know, you two have some great chemistry. He's a superstar DJ and you're the heiress in a multi-billion-dollar family. Plus, if that song takes off, he might want you to tour with him to sing it live. Heck, you should ask him to make an album with you regardless; you both have such a supreme sound."

Satellite softly reflected Ionakana's gaze then smiled at the sun. "I'll see how it goes. Gosh, he does have such a gallant glow. And as for a tour and an album, I wouldn't say no."

There, on their towels, their toned teenage bodies tanning in the sun's swath that spanned the solar system and beyond, Satellite, Ionakana and Isla savored the day like a taste of paradise in a parade on our planet's race through space where consciousness is free to evolve.

Satellite, Ionakana and Isla divvied up their still early day between diving in the warm waters of the sky-blue bay, and energetically exercising their esoteric equilibriums by flinging springing flips off the jump rock's precipice with the precision of a pendulum.

After displaying their fashionably fit flips for a while, Ionakana stood on the sandy shore and addressed the girls as they emerged from the ocean jiggling with giggles of jubilation that they bore to the core. "How about we make a move and go grab an acai bowl?"

"Yes, please!" The girls chimed together as many appreciative eyes roved over the sea salt sparkle of their bikini-clad bodies. The teen trio readily rinsed off, then grabbed their packs and walked out of Waimea Bay, where they then slapped down their boards and skated up the street, continuing their day as clean as can be.

Satellite and the siblings stopped by a super nice little shop and snagged some ice-cold acai bowls, then sat down and enjoyed them with the stories that the other patrons told. They wrapped up their short stay at the snack shop by slurping down the rest of their honey-topped sustenance, then wound their way back outside to town where they crossed the road and rock-strewn ground to the liquid quicksilver-like ebb and flow of the underwater tunnels of Shark's Cove.

It was here that the trio got their snorkeling gear out of their packs and cast a glance at the cove before Satellite closed the clasp on her pack and placed her hands on the small of her friends' backs. "Guys, I gotta say, this right here, snorkeling, the good ol' leisurely liaison between me and the aquatic creatures of creation, is quite possibly my most popular hobby." The siblings smiled, their eyes reflecting the granular sand shore that was so deeply engrained in their born and bred Hawaiian brains.

The three friends' following foray into the fresh depths of the cove was filled with swimming fish that flashed past their masks with brisk whisks of their fins. Fully in her own head under the water, Satellite's imagination ran rampant as she moved fluidly, plunging through tunnel after tunnel, each of which filled her with more and more wondrous wonder.

After swimming for only a few more minutes by flicking her fins like a dolphin, she had memorized the mesmerizing maze that was a marvelous metropolis for a myriad of magical marine species at play. Suddenly, a bump nudged her on her rump, and whirling about, her foot instinctively kicked out and gave a turtle a solid thump on the snout.

Chuckling at the young reptilian punk, Satellite surfaced, as did the turtle, where it stuck its stubby head up with a harrumph. Satellite waved an animated hand at the turtle, who slapped the water with a paddle-like flipper, making a splash, then dipped back below the ocean with a languid thrash, where it then made its lazy way for the land.

Just then, Ionakana and Isla burst forth from within one of the caves of the cove, where they then breathed in a clean lung full of air and let out a "Chee-hoo!" like a duo in tune with a secret something only they knew.

"We saw a humuhumunukunukukuapua'a in one of those underwater rooms! Man, those zany little things can zoom!" Ionakana called with a cadence from atop the crest of a tiny wave that moved the blue nuance of the ocean's soothing truth.

"I just flipper kicked a sea turtle!" Satellite boasted ebulliently as she bobbed brazenly in the beautiful blue.

The teenage trio took some time to savor the sunshine, and while treading water above the depths, they erupted into a rousing rendition of the cinematic sea chanty, 'Whale of a Tale.' They had learned the song from the classic film '20,000 Leagues under the Sea' that they had watched aboard the Lexeasure.

Swimming back ashore, Satellite, Ionakana and Isla were laughing ecstatically at the cartoon-like lyrics of the chanty. As they mounted the beach to stand on the sand, they let out a three-fold gasp as they spotted the flipper-kicked sea turtle happily flapping its fins amidst the many onlookers' sunlit grins.

"Hey! JettySet texted me!" Satellite exclaimed a minute later as she nabbed her phone from her pack.

"Ooh, what'd he say?" Isla inquired with an exquisite twist of her lips.

"He says he clicked his pop track to my songs' vocals, and he should have it ready to hit the internet as soon as he's done with all his tests and checks," Satellite replied.

Impressed with JettySet's lightning-quick work, Satellite and the siblings exchanged the look of those eager to hear the song that they knew was like thunderous luxury for the ear.

"How about we go sample some of that Banzai Skatepark action that's just a stone's throw down the road," Ionakana supplied brightly. "We can snag a shred then skip across the street and take a sunset stroll straight through the famous row of Pipeline Beach."

Leaving the flipper flapping turtle to its happy flopping, the three teens synched the chemistry between themselves with another beam of the teeth, then lit out and pelted the street with their tropical skateboarder techniques.

Banzai Skatepark was ablaze with legendary skaters going hard like untamed aliens from space. The skaters had sun-bleached hair and were flying over quarter pipe pockets without a care and a look so debonair as they rocketed off air after air.

Satellite, Ionakana and Isla strode up into the parks' trove, then roved over by the bowl, put their packs down with a little bit of show, then got the camera set on record and let it roll. They proceeded to pump the pockets with pleasure, passing the camera from person to person.

After stretching their legs and making a few acquaintances, Ionakana asked Satellite to film him get a trick he had brewing in his brimming intelligence. "I wanna hardflip between these two bubbles," Ionakana said, gesturing gracefully to two boostable concrete bubbles spaced apart a few feet. Satellite set the shot up with a very photographically composed perspective, amply capturing the spatial streamline and the athletic objective.

After many tries, Ionakana succeeded in racing around the park for speed, boosting up the bubble, popping up and flicking his foot out, snapping the trick with a clean catch, and stomping an elegant bolt landing in the curve of the other bubble.

"Ooh, Satellite, come get a clip of me carving the coping in the bowl!" Isla shouted out over the top of the cheers and applause of the skater boys making noise for Ionakana's raw sauce. Satellite perched in a prime position on the edge of the bowl and egged Isla on as she charged strong, nicking the dickens out of the lip like a pro.

"OK! My turn!" Satellite sang out. "I'll get a li'l sesh on the handrail!"

Isla gladly grabbed the camera from Satellite and assumed an artistic angle from the handrail. After a handful of attempts on the handrail, Satellite had managed to amass clips of front and backside boardslides, front and backside 50-50's, lipslides, feeble, smith and a crooked grind.

The skater boys had been going crazy watching Satellite slap down the boardslides, but the clang of the trucks on the rail for the grinds sent the boys to cloud nine. "Wow, for a girl, you've got some pretty proper prowess!" one of the wild boys exclaimed enthusiastically to Satellite's elated face.

"Everybody's dropping hammers around here!" Ionakana yelled as he unsheathed a shining shaka.

"I've got an idea!" Satellite said aside to Ionakana and Isla. "Hey! Can I get everyone together for a group photo?"

67

she called out loudly across the park to all those there. Rallying to her call, all the skater boys and even a few girls were more than happy to make an appearance in Satellite's life. Clustered together, clutching their trusty boards, and at about twenty people deep, Satellite knew this photo was a timeless peek at her adventures as a teen. The earnest enjoyment of everyone exuded the subculture effulgence of an eager team of battle-ready rapscallions. With a click, the legit picture was a hit, whereupon Satellite put it up on the internet and tagged all the kids.

"Thanks everyone! That's a keeper!" Satellite said as many amicable hands clapped her on the back. Glancing at the sky, Satellite, Ionakana and Isla huddled up as the crowd of skaters returned to their prowl of the thrill-chasing kind.

"Sunset, Pipeline Beach, let's catch it," Ionakana stated. "Absolutely," Satellite fluted. Packs grabbed, the trio dashed back out of the park's bash and onto their path.

Being that it was summer, Pipeline's swell was basically lackadaisical, with only a few of the seven-mile miracle's humdinger locals out and about ponderously perusing the usually ratchet-blasted sandy land between the quaint belle dwellings and the world-famous waves of the ocean blue.

"Geez, this beach is something fierce! Even when dormant, you can feel the power innate to this place," Ionakana commented with reverence.

"The most ferocious things are often the most fabulous too," Isla said wisely, her wide eyes piercing the perpetual prominence of the pleasant slice of paradise.

The teen triple team submerged in the salty swash, and while wading, they had a deep talk about a few existential hot topics.

"I honestly consider myself a bit of a singularitarian," Ionakana said solemnly. "Technologically speaking, humanity will exponentially advance to societal levels unimaginable with artificial intelligences and continued scientific breakthroughs. That's the technological singularity. And the natural singularities out in the cosmos are the undisputed force of the universe. Frankly, on a scale larger than we know, I think those beasts churn out new universes at a rate unfathomable. People need to place more praise on singularities."

Satellite's eyes sparkled wildly.

Ionakana continued, pouring forth over the gentle ocean's noise. "I think the greatest minds and bodies are something like the cosmos in and of themselves. Jesus, Buddha, Krishna... the celestial characters that ignited planetary culture. And then there's the minds behind Olympic athletes; so honed and toned to human perfection. I'm telling you, that's what I'm about. I stay centered on the idea that people occupy their space like stars, planets, nebulas, and singularities." Satellite and Isla soaked in Ionakana's words in the serene shallows of the shoreline sweep.

"Well, I'm a simple girl," Isla said with a little bit of a melody as she played with her hair that was upon her shoulders. "I believe in cherishing beauty and living in and for all things glorious."

"I'm full-on imagination," Satellite said seizing her turn. "I think that true creation comes from consciousness. There's only one place where that comes from and that's our brains. I say the most imaginative and creative person is fulfilling their real purpose. But you know what, I've heard of a doctrine called Lazerism, and I like it. It's all about music, dance, art, technology, and the celebration of the mysteries of the universe." Ionakana and Isla excitedly popped their eyes at this tidbit of info and shared a look.

As their conversation merged with the evening mystique of the beach, the sun set on another eventful Hawaiian day.

As the siblings talked between themselves, Satellite quietly reminisced on the whirlwind past few days for a moment as twilight overtook the sky. She felt truly blessed to have formed such a fond friendship with Ionakana and Isla, as they all foraged at such a fast pace through the fruitions of their able-bodied raving fables.

After travelling for eons through deep space, the silver starlight bathed the three dream chasers as they billowed out of the blue, grabbed their packs, and made a beeline off the beach for the bus that would take them back to the Lexeasure and their pillows kept cool.

An hour later, the trio had thanked the bus driver, walked through the wildness of Waikiki, boated over to the Lexeasure, and were now glad to be back in the grandeur of the great floating homestead. It was a little late, but by happenstance, a few crew members could be seen tending to the upkeep of the lavish cabins, rendering the trendy spaces of everyone with a clean keep.

Entering the galley with rumbles in their stomachs after a day of making musical thunder, beach running, stunning underwater chumming and skate park stunting along the front of the North Shore jungle, the fridge looked like a puzzle of wonder for their hunger.

Filling up their plates with food and their glasses with lilikoi juice, Satellite, Ionakana and Isla ceremoniously seated themselves at the table and said grace before heartily digging in and quaffing down their juice with impish grins and dribbles going down their ridgeline chins.

Just then, Satellite's phone sounded out a text message tone. "It's JettySet! The song is live!" Satellite sang out in that surprisingly insight inducing voice she had.

"Ooh! It's up! Play the track!" Isla shrieked.

"Hang on, let's do this right," Satellite said. "Let's finish our dinners, then head out to the hot tub and play it over the speaker system."

In an instant, their plates were clean, and they were shooting up the stairs and through a hatch out to the upper aft deck. Seconds later, they were dipped in the bubbling tub with the song queued up and ready to run. Like an audio avalanche, a burning earworm suddenly descended upon them from the speakers. Satellite's angelic vocal femininity ignited the three teens' minds with an intrepid clarity, while JettySet's viscous laser disc rips mixed with gargantuan gorilla flexes of trippy bass kicks slammed on the track like a neon palette attack.

"Oh my freaking gosh!" Ionakana announced in absolute astonishment.

"This is as sick as the ichor that flows through the veins of golden gods!" Isla belted out as Satellite head banged like a velvety video vixen.

Satellite, Ionakana and Isla had the volume maxed out as they blasted JettySet and Satellite's "Smile of My Mind's Eye" on repeat as they stayed at anchor with their auras boiling and their sights on the bright nighttime skyline of Hawaii. Later they mercifully morphed like quantum quarks back to their cozy cabins, their dreams raging on like the relentless rays of their soulful sun-filled days.

Chapter 6
JettySet's Alma Mater

Three days passed in which "Smile of My Mind's Eye" blew up like a nuclear bomb on the internet. With the play count already in the double-digit millions, pop culture was happy to let the song steadily filter in. Satellite, Ionakana and Isla were spending the afternoon online in the salon aboard the Lexeasure watching what was aptly described by Ionakana as a "constantly detonating explosion", as an endless stream of music lovers discovered the sumptuous savagery of the song.

"Do you think JettySet will ask you to sing the song live with him at shows, or do you think he'll just play it?" Isla inquired. Satellite pensively put her chin to her palm as she contemplated this.

"Like I said earlier, you need to see if he'd be in to do an album with you," Ionakana said looking over from the computer, where Satellite's name was spreading like wildfire.

Just then, Satellite's phone rang out, putting a pause on the three teens' reflections and speculations.

"Oh, it's JettySet!" Satellite said happily as she swiped her finger on the phone to answer it then held it up to her ear.

"Hey JettySet! Yeah, I'm doing great! Yep, we've been watching it skyrocket for the past few days. Uh huh. Really? What? A music video?"

Ionakana and Isla were fist pumping the air with fireworks in their eyes as they beamed at Satellite.

"Yes, that sounds fantastic! Let me know when you hear more about it… OK… sounds good, talk to you later, see ya!" Satellite hung up her phone and gaped with a bedazzled face at Ionakana and Isla.

"A music video!" she squealed. "Here, come with me! I gotta find Granddad and Grandmother and tell them the news of my music!"

The two young ladies and the lad poked around the luxurious labyrinth of the floating home before discovering the grandparents lunching under an umbrella on the upper deck alone.

Bobbing up to the lunch-munching couple, Satellite lovingly clapped her hands together and held them in a prayerful position while Isla and Ionakana flanked her in her thankful state.

"Granddad, Grandmother, JettySet just called and said they want to film a music video for my song!" Satellite frothed out. "Oh, my word, dear!" Grandmother exclaimed with surprise. "What a beautiful opportunity to showcase your myriads of merry talents!"

"I like the sound of this JettySet boy," Granddad stated proudly. "Your Grandmother and I looked up his music, and goodness does it pack a punch. When does he want to film the video?" Granddad continued.

"As soon as possible," Satellite said earnestly.

"Well," Granddad said gently pausing, "We were actually getting ready to tell you this. I just received news that we had the finishing touches put on a new product for Omnikinetica by our…" Granddad paused again, smiling and adding a twinkling wink, "… top scientists. We're raising anchor in a day for a voyage to the Sacavage family headquarters. You visited when you were a very little girl. We've had some development since, but you know the place - Blue Island, Bahamas."

"Well, that sounds wonderful, but what about the music video?" Satellite asked feeling taken aback in light of her blossoming opportunity. "This is my chance to make a name for myself, Granddad."

"I have a film crew on the island with state-of-the-art equipment. Why don't you invite JettySet on our voyage and get to know your collaborator? I daresay I've got a prized surprise for you there that would take your music video to a whole new level," Granddad flashed his famous smile. "Don't you worry, Satellite, we've got your best interests at heart, we'll take care of all the variables," Granddad said nodding solemnly.

Relief swept Satellite's face. "Is it OK if Ionakana and Isla stay with us? I'd like for them to be in the music video," Satellite asked.

"Of course, dear," the Grandparents said in unison, chuckling as they did so. "Why don't you invite JettySet, and call Mr. and Mrs. Iden and ask if they're OK with a vacation inside of a vacation for their children?" Granddad said, taking a sip of his white wine, effectively wrapping up the conversation.

The arrangements were all made by later that afternoon. Mr. and Mrs. Iden were thrilled to hear that Satellite wanted Ionakana and Isla in her music video, and that their children were travelling the world.

JettySet was beside himself with Peter Pan aplomb at Satellite's suggestion that he accompany them on the voyage to the Caribbean for the video shoot on the Sacavage's private island.

"With such a long voyage in front of us," JettySet had told Satellite over the phone, "I'm for sure going to bring my recording equipment and laptop, so we can churn out some more juicy tunes. Heck, we might even get a full-fledged album out of this!"

Ionakana and Isla had dashed off on a mall outing to Ala Moana Shopping Center to pick up some more fresh clothes as their parents had only packed a few fashionable fits for them, and they wanted a few more to flash about in for the Caribbean.

The countdown wound down until everyone was in, safe and sound from town and settling in around Granddad's renowned crown jewel, the Lexeasure, top of the yachting mound of holy ground.

Gathered together in the literary luminosity of the library, a light-hearted Granddad addressed Satellite, JettySet, Ionakana and Isla about a captivating matter that had him happy as a clam on the verge of laughter.

"Now I know all of you are wondering why I'm keeping secrets about what I've got on Blue Island, but I stand firm in 'seeing-is-believing' and the exhilarating embrace of a sensational 'sweeping-off-the-feet'. The product that my 'top scientists' have just completed and thoroughly tested is going to revolutionize society, and at the cusp of its release, I think you all and your music video would be the perfect way to unveil it to the world. I guarantee you're going to like it. That's all I want to say about it for now, but I think you'll have a one-of-a-kind piece of art when this is all said and done." Granddad stood proudly before the youngsters, the comfortable fragrance of the books peacefully wafting through the air.

Then with a jubilant wink, he nodded goodnight and cruised out of the library.

"Wow, your Granddad has me all riled up to see what this surprise is," JettySet said keenly. "I'm glad he understands the artistic nature of our work, and that he sees our video as a big enough vessel for this new enigmatic product."

"I'm excited to see what this new product is too," Satellite said dreamily from amidst the backdrop of books. "And the Caribbean is a straight eye candy place for video visuals." Satellite stared into space for a moment with a whimsical look on her face. "We've got a plush combo multiplier going and I've got a mountainous fountain of lyrical ideas flowing. I once heard the expression 'future nostalgia', and if this isn't full immersion in that, then I don't know what is."

Ionakana and Isla giggled appreciatively. "You know," Isla said looking from the book-lined walls to the group, "being surrounded by all this knowledge reminded me that Ionakana and I start college at the end of the summer at University of Hawaii at Manoa." Looking now at Satellite, Isla continued, "I know you said you were still thinking your future over. But you just had a new avenue open for you with this song. You could potentially break out as an artist. Do you think you could balance that with college or a career?"

Satellite thought this over for a moment, then just as she was about to respond, JettySet spoke.

"I think it's time I tell you where that turquoise tiger tooth necklace came from."

Satellite craned her neck around to get a good look at JettySet.

"I made it at the college I went to for my bachelor's degree," JettySet's voice trailed off as he glimpsed his recent past. Resuming his train of thought with a renewed vigor and courage he continued. "I went to the notorious Kaimana Hoku School of Visionary Consciousness on Hawaii's Big Island. A school so steeped in the creative arts that many students are forced to leave because of the crushing demand of the program. It's a rigorous combination of extremely imaginative physical trials as well as the responsibility of producing absolutely inspired original work on a daily basis for four years."

Satellite, Ionakana and Isla stared wide-eyed in awe at JettySet. "You... you went to Kaimana Hoku?" Satellite said shocked. "That's one of the most arduous colleges in the world."

"Yes, yes, it is," JettySet said in a stone-cold tone. "But if you want to be an artist in your respected field, there's no better school. With that being said, if we can make an album and you wholeheartedly want to pursue being an artist, that's where you need to go."

Satellite's mind raced. Suddenly, she could see the beautiful future she had been dreaming of. The one she had glimpsed from the turquoise tiger tooth necklace. The one where she brazenly blasted up her own path, free to unleash her unfettered stream of creative ideas from the hallowed halls of a school that perfectly encapsulated one of her biggest life's desires; to bestow unto others a bona fide bop of her otherworldly spiritual energy.

"But if Satellite puts an album out and goes on tour, how will she have time for class?" Ionakana asked JettySet.

"Oh, Kaimana Hoku absolutely works in budding artists' projects to the school semester schedule," JettySet said reassuringly.

Satellite smoothly emerged from her thoughts and said to the others, "I've been looking for a way to make my own name in this world. A way to stand up as myself among my self-made family. My song blowing up, the opportunity to film a video and make an album with a superstar DJ like JettySet, the challenge of an auspicious art school; I feel like destiny is illuminating these steps for me." Satellite now turned to look directly at JettySet. "First thing tomorrow, let's get a jump on the next song. I must have gushed out a dozen luscious lyrical wonders in my notepad. I'm ready if you are."

JettySet smiled, his eyes glittering with fast-paced fantastic futures amongst the library's laid-back literary movements.

That night, while in her room, Satellite got a text. Checking it, she saw that it was from JettySet. "Meet me on the upper deck, I'd like to talk," it said.

Satellite, curious, moved out of her room and made her way up through the vast luxurious labyrinth of the Lexeasure. A moment later, she strode across the star-lit upper deck towards a silhouetted JettySet, who, in the Lexeasure's mood lighting, had on a diamond chain that seemed to be strobing.

"Hey, what's up?" Satellite asked.

"I just wanted to take a minute to get to know you a little better," JettySet said. "I feel like we're still strangers, and if I'm going to take this voyage with you, and make an album with you, I'd like to consider you as more than an acquaintance."

"Oh. Fair enough," Satellite said seeing the reasoning behind him.

"I guess I'll start off simple," JettySet said. "What's your favorite color?"

Satellite smiled. "Honestly, that varies depending on the shade, the saturation, the context, the pop, the time of day, the lighting… you can't pin me with one color; I'm a full-spectrum kind of girl."

"Shoots, OK. Where you from?"

"Well, I was born in North Carolina, but I was raised in Switzerland because my parents worked on the CERN particle accelerator."

"Whoa, now that's pretty awesome. How about… what are your favorite pastimes?"

"Oh, the list is long. I love everything under the sun. But I guess my favorites are friends, family, adventure, board sports, the ocean, the mountains, music, photography, movies, fitness, art, poetry, shoes, fashion, space, and living to find enlightenment in all I do."

"That's a proper good list," JettySet said impressed. "I might have listed almost all the same things for myself. How about brothers and sisters? Or are you an only child?"

"Only child," Satellite said. "I always wanted to have a brother and a sister, but I guess being an only child helped me reach out and make friends pretty easily."

"I noticed that. You are pretty personable," JettySet complimented.

"What about you?" Satellite asked. "Only child?"

"I have two brothers, Flynn and Finian."

Satellite laughed. "A nice little Faleafine frenzy." Florian smiled. "We're solid. You got a car?"

"Oh no, I drove one of my parents' cars in Switzerland, and now I'm staying with my grandparents here in Hawaii, so no car."

"Oh, I guess that leads to my next question," JettySet said.

"How long are you going to stay with your grandparents?"

"Well, my parents got called to work on a classified job. It's not supposed to be a forever thing. And I am supposed to start college after the summer… still not sure where I'm going… but I like the sound of that Kaimana Hoku School you went to. I'm going to ask if I can do a late entry. I'd love for my schooling and my passions to run side by side."

"Absolutely. With talent like yours, you'd be out of place everywhere else but at Kaimana Hoku."

JettySet adjusted his diamond chain. Satellite's eyes sparkled. "How about food? You got favorites?" he asked.

"Oh. Just you wait. Now that you're with the Sacavage's, you're going to feast on some meals like you wouldn't believe. Grandmother can cook like a recipe textbook," Satellite said comically rubbing her skinny stomach.

JettySet chuckled.

"Oh, here's one. Tell me about your singing voice. Surely you must notice that it's pretty peculiar. I mean, it sounds like it's coming from somewhere else besides you. Like you're channeling it through yourself from some other world or something."

Satellite said nothing for a second.

"I just have it like that," she said thoughtfully. "I have a vision. Sometimes it seems like some presence other than me is guiding my sight, helping me do what is right."

"Well, it's incredible. It's a golden ticket. And I promise I can put tracks down that will amplify your sound profound and put you on straight up holy ground."

"Yeah, about that, your music, it's so distinct," Satellite said. "How did you develop that sound that you have?"

"Oh baby, where do I even begin?" JettySet said sizing up

Satellite and the sky. "It's a supernatural by-product of living so truthfully, so unapologetically, so unfettered in my pursuit of what I love, that it just comes so easily because I am it. My hands touch the tech, and I just distill the intrinsic licks and riffs of my vision's exponential lift."

They both were silent for a moment under the stars. "You got a boyfriend?" JettySet asked innocently.

Satellite smiled slowly, "Noo... I've actually only had friends that were boys, but never a boyfriend."

They were silent for another moment. "Why do you ask?" Satellite asked.

"Well, if we're going to be working so closely together... Just checking I suppose..."

Satellite laughed softly.

"I think this is going to work out very well," Satellite said. "You and me. I think this collaboration is perfect. And our meeting..." she laughed. "Now that was something else." She smiled knowingly.

"Agreed," JettySet said solidly. "Well, I say we get to work first thing tomorrow. I'm glad we caught up real quick just one-on-one."

Satellite looked happily at JettySet. " . I think we've got something extraordinary we can bring to the world." She glanced at the stars. "Well, goodnight, I'll see you bright and early."

"Goodnight." JettySet said, drinking in every drop of the scene.

Chapter 7
Voyaging Full Volume

The Lexeasure was well underway, slicing through the heavenly Hawaiian waters headed in the direction of the warm shallow seas of the Caribbean, by the time Satellite, the siblings, and JettySet happily roused and proudly crowded in the salon, eager now to hound out a loud sound that had some serious glossy pop and pow.

In a whirlwind, Satellite whipped out her notepad and donned the headphones that were connected to JettySet's laptop, where he cycled through some of his thick and thugging sonic scenes.

Upon finding a particularly rich-clipped grizzly bear hit, Satellite plucked her courage, flawlessly formed herself into a flume of that otherworldly deep see-through truth, and sprayed out a full sun-soaked ceremony of a song so ornamented in opulent ocular oases that it scythed the senses with a sharp, swinging rambunctious rhythm.

With a swift gifted lick, Satellite knocked out every segment of the song in one confident clutch of love after another. With a final purr, she finished the song and JettySet immediately saved it. Shining with the sunny security that only singing a heartfelt song can produce, Satellite stated simply, "Sea Spray Face — that's what I call that song."

The siblings bobbed like baubles applauding Satellite's laudable song, talking strong amongst themselves with oblong smiles spread along their honest and raw faces that were no façade.

"Now I'll tell you right here," Satellite said, "I'm singing my most easy-to-flow-with songs first. I'm saving the more lyrically tricky ones for last. Those might take a few takes."

"Satellite," JettySet said, passing her a steadfast glance, "wherever it is that you're coming from in these songs, stand that ground. You've got this. Just pour your heart forward with purity onto the pounding palette of the track; and don't worry, we can always run it back."

Smiling, and holding JettySet's gaze for a long moment, Satellite serenely steered herself back into her mysterious state, whereupon JettySet set to sampling a few sonically silken selections for her next song.

Upon hearing the one she wanted, Satellite held up a finger and JettySet started the recording countdown. Satellite sounded sage-like as she sang in lucid lyrics about a path that was populated with laughing travelers, questing about in the beauty of nature for spiritual enlightenment and the divine insight of happily ever after.

It was a jubilant jaunt of a song, and after Satellite had brought it to a halt on an exalted seashore awash with salt, she concluded the pop romp with a dive into the whitewash.

"The Laughing Path," Satellite said smoothly winking and hanging out her tongue. "Next track, I'm on fire."

Her next song certainly was fire, as it was the sun itself that she serenaded. Her valiant verses gilded with godly gleans guided the other three through sunlit visual vistas, artistically enhanced with blissful beautiful movements and the teenage dream of finding meaning in all you see.

With the last long and strong note of the song, Satellite

seemed to sweep the squad's spirits back into their bodies after the solar soul throw that her versatile vocals had shown them how to know the way to go.

Satellite sighed smiling and sat down lithely.

"Nice one!" Ionakana said with pleasure. "I feel like I'm watching a movie behind my eyelids when you sing."

"Yeah," Isla agreed. "They need to test you for alien DNA 'cuz I can't figure out where it is you're coming from with these songs." Isla winked cheekily and asked, "By the way, what's that one called?"

"Mmm, that's Sunshine Science," Satellite said, humbly hunching her shoulders and looking at her feet for a moment. Then she proudly reared back and glanced out the glass doors.

"How about we take a break for breakfast?" JettySet posed hopefully.

"Sounds good," Satellite said, returning her gaze to the others. "The next song requires some deeper emotions. A quick bite to eat might help bolster my volition into motion and lower my inhibitions so I can really go in."

The youthful group smoothly glided into the galley and set straight to perusing the room for some suitable breakfast food. Satellite, who was lost in thought on her songs, absent-mindedly grabbed a grapefruit instead of an orange with her yogurt. As the others laughed in amusement, Satellite let loose a lip-puckered "Oof", as she squinted with the extremely tart taste bud shock.

Settling in at the table, everybody tucked in with the siblings having decided on a box of cereal, and JettySet on a couple of energy bars.

Satellite remained reserved as she thoughtfully pondered her songs while JettySet and the siblings happily crafted carefree scenarios of tootling through the beauteous room of the idyllic Blue Island's views during the day, and under the soothing hues from the light of the upcoming full moon.

Turning to Satellite from the group's amusing musings, Isla asked gently, "If you don't mind me asking, what's the song about that's got you so absorbed?"

Satellite came to a little bit, and delicately avoiding JettySet's gaze, offered somewhat vaguely, "Well, boys really. It's a song about some boys I know."

JettySet and Ionakana shifted slightly in their seats, respectfully inspecting Satellite with intrigue and supportive belief.

"Oh!" Isla said smiling wide. "I see. Don't be too bashful with the boys. Plus, you're the new artist here, we're here to reinforce you as you freely explore your creative expressions."

Satellite beamed appreciatively.

"Thank you. Honestly, I just want to do justice to them. Seeing these boys in action is one of the things that inspires me to do the things I do."

JettySet and Ionakana shared a look then nodded at Satellite. "Well, listen," Satellite continued, "I feel better now that I opened that up. Let's finish up in here then go knock another song out."

JettySet, Isla and Ionakana laughed happily at this and cleared the table with a fresh pep in their step.

Despite her ruminations, Satellite relished revealing the revelations of radical boys as she belted out her beloved emotions with brobdingnagian magic over the top of JettySet's galaxy-grinding, lightning strike and thunderclap track.

Though Satellite was whole-heartedly confessing her affection for the boys in her life in her lyrics, which Ionakana and JettySet heard mention of themselves, the group stayed steadfast as Satellite's open soul captured the captivating admirations of fully-charmed crush gushes.

Even though Satellite had said this song might take a few tries to get right, she plowed through courageously first try and concluded beautifully with a cherry-on-top air smooch "Mwah!" on the fly.

The Lexeasure salon rang out in applause as the grounded and astounded gang cheered Satellite's vocal victory and the astonishing sonic tonic of her idolized icons of life.

From amid the happily complimented boys, Isla delightfully inquired, "Oh Satellite, bravo! So perfectly put! What's the title of that one?"

Satellite, smiling, peered with purity at each of the three in turn, then replied brightly, "Don't Look Away."

Over the top of the buzz brewing between them all, Satellite, feeling quite chuffed, confidently raised her right hand and said, "I need to rest my voice. We can pick this back up tomorrow. How about a dip in the pool, so we can sponge up some sun?"

Satellite, Isla, Ionakana and JettySet were all serene smiles as they slipped into their rooms, slid into their swimsuits, and regrouped by the cool blue pool that looked like a jewel.

The endless ocean stretched in all directions around them as they submerged in the liquid church-like space that purged them of all their hurts, while gleans of infinity from the horizon ignited their desire to quench their every physical, emotional, and spiritual thirst.

Each of the four friends savored the sight of each other's delightfully fine, tight, kind, bright, laser line bodies as they swam in the sun light.

Amidst the playful pandemonium of the pool, the same refractions of attraction that had emanated from JettySet's eye at Starnectar once again covered Satellite like honey with a hilarious graciousness.

Satellite's eyes flicked over and met JettySet's for the briefest of moments. And in that moment, the swell of that celestial syzygy surged once more and a longing showed clear as day on both their faces.

Between the sphinx and the sheik, a wanton want had erupted.

Satellite and JettySet both composed themselves cordially with poise amidst the noise, but their hearts were racing and the thought of tasting each other's lips had chased blazing so amazing between their gently drop-jawed faces.

Letting the burning yearning sink in, Satellite, wearing a mischievous grin, softly began talking atop the waters' chop to a rock solid statuesque JettySet, who had his thick wet hair tousled up quite a lot.

"So, Florian, can I call you Florian?"

With a steadfast gaze and a smile spreading across his fine face, Florian allowed Satellite's playful ploy to disarm him of his professional pseudonym.

"Yes," Florian said with tranquility, taking nothing for granted as he peacefully let his eyes play with Satellite's gorgeous red-orange hair and the fine frenzy that were her many faceted flashy photogenic features.

"What is it that you want most in life?" Satellite asked with her eyes locked on his.

Florian didn't hesitate to herald her with his answer.

"Aside from the joys of inspiring people with music,

travelling the world and unraveling cultures, living with aloha in Hawaii, and rising through society, there is one paramount point that is pivotal in my rigorously disciplined life."

Both their locked eyes were now smiling as Florian paused flawlessly in his flow to the answer that Satellite knew she was already in the know.

"The slipstream of sanctity," Florian said feeling Satellite's unspoken acknowledgment. "I look at the big picture and let my spirit swim in the ocean of the omniverse," Florian nodded. "And then you found one of my tributes to The All. The turquoise tiger tooth necklace."

Satellite, stunned in the sun, checked the necklace that still adorned her chest.

Florian continued, "I would ask what it is you want most in life, but since you've been to Kalalau, it seems we are both literally and figuratively on the same path."

"Well, you should still ask me," Satellite said.

"Of course, my apologies, I shouldn't assume," Florian replied.

After a momentary pause, and now with the attention of the siblings on them, Florian asked, "Satellite, what is it you want out of all of this?"

Satellite, wading up to her waist in the cool blue bejeweled pool, touched all ten of her fingertips together.

"I want to create something that benefits all mankind and is a perfect reflection of my personality that can survive in society as a treasured heritage piece for my family for all future time to come. That's what I want," she finished with a stark solidness.

The siblings looked incredulously between Satellite and Florian, as they had just become privy to the increasingly deep, intimacy-tinted connection developing there.

Florian looked skyward for a second, taking a breath of the breeze, then feeling relieved to have heard her deepest dream, gave her his gaze from her feet to her face pristine.

"You're in it with all your being, and with that angel-from-another-world voice you have, you can absolutely attain your vision one in the same."

The siblings concurred with Florian, which calmly concluded the conversation.

Everyone's sunny sensations seemed to converge, diverting their luxurious urges from the cool blue bejeweled pool as they emerged from it in an energetic surge with no need for words and a desire to quench their thirst.

Just then, as if their thoughts had carried through the air, Grandmother came through the glass salon doors clutching four ice cold bottles of lilikoi kombucha.

"Just thought you all could do for some icy swigs," she said, softly chuckling as she handed the ice-cold bottles to the four friends.

"We're on the upper deck if you need anything. Your Granddad is going to be busy coordinating the release of his new product, so best let him be." Grandmother warmly smiled lovingly at them. "Oh, you all make just the cutest little group. I'm excited to see what you think of being free on the beach on our little island slice."

She winked at Satellite, then breezed back into the salon and out of sight.

"I wonder what on earth it is that your Granddad is going to release," Ionakana said solemnly. "He said it's going to change society."

"You know," Satellite pondered puckishly, "We might just

be able to find that out."

"Whoa now, what do you mean?" Isla inquired anxiously. "Shouldn't we just wait 'til we get to Blue Island and your Granddad shows us?"

"Well…" Satellite said slowly, with the tiniest of impish twists in her lips. "We could just dip our toes in, know what I mean? Do a bit of smooth sleuthing… even just a keyword would sate my curiosity," Satellite now split into a full-fledged roguish smile. "Now, I will be clear on this, though," she said seriously. "I will never betray the trust of Granddad, and I will not disturb his lab… but," she giggled gregariously, "If I got everyone together for a group photo, and recommended we use Granddad's phone for the photo, I could 'accidentally' open the texts and have a window of about five seconds to scour the messages for a keyword."

The anxiety of the others dissolved at Satellite's wholesome hoodwink.

"Oh, well that doesn't seem so bad," Isla said with relief. "This wild whimsy is all yours though," Isla continued, "I think I speak for us three as guests that we don't want to tarnish our invitation to be aboard the Lexeasure."

"Oh, you guys are fine," Satellite said, "to be honest, Granddad likes those that take initiative. He'd probably get a real kick out of this little scheme."

"Your grandmother said he'd be busy all day. When is a good time to activate this slightly slippery scenario?" Florian inserted inquisitively.

"Dinner time," Satellite said solidly. "I'll just catch them and ask if I can send a photo of everyone to my mom and dad. I know it'll be odd for me to take the picture, but I'll just say it's an update on yacht life from my perspective. Then boom!

Fast as a laser blast, I'll see if I can get a keyword."

Satellite shook out her mango maroon mane and touched her tongue to her teeth with a tomboyish flourish.

"Well, we've got some time 'til dinner, I'd kinda like to gloss over those songs and pop some of my trademark stars on the bars," Florian said, eyeing his laptop visible through the salon's glass doors.

"This Lexeasure life is awesome!" Ionakana said, speaking for the first time in a while. "Cruising, talking story, wil'n out, all the main staples of some real aloha livin'!"

The four friends whiled away the afternoon in the salon, with Florian working his berserker wizardry on Satellite's prodigious songs.

Around dinner time, Satellite, assuming Granddad would take a break from work and accompany Grandmother to the galley where they'd whip up some grub, called them on the intercom.

"Hey Grandmother, Granddad, I was wondering if before dinner we could all get together and I could take of picture of everyone to send to Mom and Dad." Even though this was a completely innocent request, the four friends waited with bated breath at the prospect of this little hoodwink.

"Oh Satellite, that'd be nice. Where do you want to meet?" Grandmother chimed back over the intercom.

"How 'bout the very tip top of the bow?" Satellite posed.

"All right dear, see you in a few," Grandmother said brightly as the intercom clicked off.

"Okee dokee, let's go guys. I'll have about five seconds to see if I can snag that keyword," Satellite said as she broke into a fit of girlish giggles. "Granddad would get a real kick out of this if he knew what I was up to."

A moment later, the friends exited the front hatch to the lavish expanse of the Lexeasure's bow. The grandparents were already standing prominently at the furthest most point of the yacht.

As the four friends strode forward, Satellite threw a hilarious wink of tomfoolery at Isla, Ionakana and Florian. Their faces shone with more amusement than usual as they approached the genial grandparents.

"All right, let's snap this baby," Granddad said barrel-chested as they all congregated at the tip top of the bow.

"I wanna take the picture," Satellite said, unable to hide a wink. "I'd like to show everyone from my point of view."

"Fair enough," Granddad piped up proudly, eyeing everything in sight.

"Oh shoots! Would you believe it? I forgot my phone!" Satellite exclaimed over the sound of the ocean, still unable to hide her chic wink. "Granddad, can I take the shot on your phone?"

"Absolutely," Granddad said, charmed as always by his granddaughter.

Granddad handed the phone over, and with Isla, Ionakana and Florian knowing what to look for, saw her fingers fly almost imperceptibly over the surface of the phone.

Barely had an elongated moment passed when Satellite sang out, "Got it!" She turned the phone around and displayed a delightful photo of all of them with the massive superstructure of the Lexeasure behind them.

"Very nice, I'll send that straight-away to your parents," Granddad said, happily taking the phone gently back from Satellite.

"Dinner will be ready in no time," Grandmother said

fondly to the four friends. "I'll call when it's time."

The Grandparents sauntered off across the bow and back into the vaulted hallway.

Isla, Ionakana and Florian spun around on the spot and all chorused, "Well!"

"It's called 'The Erusaexel Suit'," Satellite said with a smile as bright as the sun that was setting directly into her fetching young face.

Dinner was a very pleasant affair that evening. The four friends kept exchanging cheeky furtive looks over their pepper steaks while Satellite maintained a constant conversation with Granddad in hopes of learning more about their burning question, "What was the Erusaexel Suit?"

Granddad was set on his secrecy though, and having obtained no more information to entertain their brains, the entire ensemble enjoyed their desert of banana pudding cups and continued putting their own ideas together on what the Suit could be.

Satellite volunteered to clean up the galley after dinner and bid goodnight to the grandparents as they amicably retired to their master suite on the fourth deck.

As the four friends tidied up under the soothing mood lights, suddenly Florian straightened and looked Satellite in the eyes.

"Wait a second!" he exclaimed with a realization dawning on him. "Erusaexel is Lexeasure backwards!"

Satellite, Isla and Ionakana stopped what they were doing in a state of suspension at this auspicious apprehension.

"Oh my gosh! Why didn't I see that immediately?" Satellite said surprised.

"What does that even mean?" Isla inquired. "Is Lexeasure

93

just a fancy word, or is it a real thing?"

Satellite pondered the stars through the ceiling for a moment before responding.

"The Lexeasure is Granddad's word. It's everything he stands for. He created it by amalgamating lexicon and treasure. A lexicon is the complete set of meaningful units in a language. Granddad believes that every word and every action should be directed towards discovering the treasures of life."

Florian, Isla and Ionakana looked at Satellite in awe as she continued.

"The Erusaexel Suit. Maybe it's some kind of suit that embodies his belief in some way. His company Omnikinetica is all futuristic technology. Maybe it's a suit integrated with a computer? That sounds plausible…"

"Dang, that's some pretty deductive reasoning, Satellite," Ionakana said honestly. "Now that you've said it, I'd be willing to bet it's something like that."

"Ooh, I hope it's form-fitting and comes in the full spectacular spectrum of colorways!" Isla exclaimed eagerly.

Satellite laughed out loud.

"Knowing Granddad's outstanding appreciation of abstract aesthetics, I'm sure he has a whole team of designers that drafted out downright delicious depictions of Lexeasure living."

Feeling pleased that their little scheme had allowed them to sneak a peek through the keyhole of Granddad's realized dream, the four friends exchanged beaming smiles with their clean teeth under the gleaming lights of the ceiling. Then they gushed out of the galley happily back to their lavish cabins, ready for sleep's dream sequences that were equal to the flawlessly dauntless discoveries of the days they were being, seeing, and fully believing in.

Chapter 8
The Erusaexel Suit

The Lexeasure's voyage cruised beautifully atop the Pacific for about a fortnight before shooting through the locks of the Panama Canal, and then streaming free into the sapphire seas of the Caribbean.

Satellite and Florian stayed a blur as they churned out burning track after track with Isla and Ionakana chipping in with harmonious backing. Satellite's song list now included new tunes like: "Horizon's Light", "Star Soul", "True Views from a Blue Moon", "Lifted in Glyphs", "Electro Escape", "Pop Out Atop the Canopy", "Bathing in the Cascade", "Passion Fashion", and "Creature Comforts".

Satellite, Florian, Isla and Ionakana had even gone down to the lower deck and introduced the music to the crew, to absolute booming enthusiasm. Even the captain had come down and enjoyed the lush, scrumptious, lovely music of Satellite's album.

The warm Caribbean seas teemed with other boats full up with ensembles audibly waving salutations as they welcomed the Lexeasure to the elated celebrations of the islands' lively cultural appreciation.

Their voyage ventured forward with vestal vim passing Jamaica, then Cuba. With grins spread from Satellite's hymns and a strong desire for a good Caribbean swim, everybody breathed a sigh of relief as they entered into the Bahamas with

Blue Island only a short way away, where they would pull in for the win and settle straight in.

And there it was, lo and behold, Blue Island, a bedazzling diamond of an island, swathed in sapphire. Over the years, Granddad had developed his tiny private island into something of an exclusive esoteric epicenter for epicureans, and a bit of a spiritual retreat for high minded clientele which he had aptly named 'Sunstone Sanctuary'.

Apart from the luxurious bliss of his gorgeous resort on the northern Bravery Beach, Granddad had also built a few facilities just down the road from the main home where several staff worked in secret on some of his most searing-edge software and tailor-made technology. Of course, the island also boasted some coastal forest, the beautiful and secluded Wade Bay, and even a small airfield on the western side.

The gargantuan gestalt of the Lexeasure gunned one last time to finish its run, then purred as it pulled into its mooring offshore in the depths just outside the shallows where the day's rays illuminated small waves making their way into Wade Bay.

Despite the anticipation to get ashore, everyone kept a good display of decorum as their eyes danced from the decorated Lexeasure to the fanciful forum of tasteful pleasures upon Blue Island's marvelous measure of shores.

After boating everyone over to the small wooden dock at Wade Bay with their loads stowed aboard, a team of resort employees with slides on their feet greeted them happily as they squealed in clean to the beach for pickup as part of the island's golf cart fleet.

Amidst the gentle hustle and bustle of everybody getting on the golf carts, Florian let his eyes slide from the sky to the surf to Satellite standing on the sand and pointedly proclaimed,

"This little island is such a glistening Elysian vision. It's a light slice of what my mind sees when I listen to your rhythms."

Everybody turned at Florian's words, marveling at the chemistry sparkling honestly so strongly it seemed even godly.

With everybody busy feeling new life in Blue Island's vibes, Granddad cleared his throat brightly. "Now, I purposefully named the road ahead to home 'Conch Shell Court', so I could say this catch phrase: 'To the Conch'!" At this, Granddad burst out in brass laughing at himself.

After a brief careen up Conch Shell Court, everyone was feeling keen to see the island home Granddad had named, "The Conch". As the picturesque white house came into view, Satellite's eyes widened at a familiar sight.

"Mom! Dad!" Satellite exclaimed. Sure as the sun, Satellite's parents waved at everyone from the entrance of the Conch's inviting front.

With a whip of the wheel, all the carts formed a formation out of formality in the front yard, where everything was just so extraordinary.

Ruby hued hair tossed back with a blossom blooming on her smooth youthful face, Satellite ran up and hugged her lovable parents all in good grace.

"What on earth is going on? What are you guys doing here?" Satellite asked, as she latched happily on her Dad's arm.

"Oh baby, do we have a secret to tell you," he said.

"Hold your horses there, Saros! We'll get to the secret telling all in good time. We're going to do the unveiling in the light of the lab," Granddad admitted brickishly as he dismounted the golf cart and strode over, placing a boulderous hand on Saros's shoulder. "Kids, this is my son, Saros,

Satellite's dad."

Florian, Isla and Ionakana waved hello to the tall, tan, rock solid figure that was Satellite's father. Saros was a primal, earthly-looking man in incredible shape with ocean blue eyes that seemed to be looking at all the answers of the cosmos. He also seemed to adhere to a very stylish sense of fashion; an urbane look that said: "I'm barely tame", completed by a machine clean shaved head that was keeping a perfect hairline at bay.

With a nourishing flourish, Granddad stepped sideways and proudly placed his palms on both biceps of the wild and wonderous woman beside Saros that was the chic peak of mystique.

"And this," Granddad said to the three friends, "is Satellite's magnificent mother, Sage." Sage Sacavage's beauty was surreal, like a painted portrait from another world. Florian, Isla and Ionakana could see where Satellite got her sphinx-like visage from. And there, upon Sage's heavenly head, were the thick, rich, luscious locks so raspberry, they simply screamed of her hair's vitality of being.

Satellite looked lovingly at her mother and said with reverence, "Mom, these are my friends. Isla and Ionakana Iden, the brother and sister twins from Hanalei, Kauai." Mrs. Sacavage nodded in greeting.

"And this," Satellite said shining with phenomenal futuristic vigor, "is Florian Faleafine, better known as JettySet, my celebrity DJ guiding light and producer that creates all the musical movements of my songs' beautiful tunes."

"Florian, pleasure to meet you. We've heard some of your hits on the radio. Such success so young. You must stay busy," Mrs. Sacavage said with a worldly wisdom way in her words.

"Yes ma'am," Florian said. "I'm proud to say Satellite and I made a whole album on the Lexeasure that is only 'The Sound'. All killer, no filler is the niche specific."

Mr. Sacavage perked his eyebrows in supreme interest, looking extremely pleased with Satellite and Florian as Florian continued. "After her first song, 'Smile of My Mind's Eye' erupted online, my record label encouraged me to produce her music. Lyrically, vocally, and sonically, I think we can inspire such a vast audience. And of course, with hit songs comes an astronomical amount of money, the thrill of live show touring, and the versatility of having a career and lifestyle based purely on passion."

"Oh, Satellite! Your stars are aligning!" Mrs. Sacavage said, beautifully viewing her daughter at this news. "You've always wanted to make your own way in this world with nothing but your heart's fire."

For the first time in quite a while, Grandmother chimed in. "Well now, I know what the secret is we're keeping, and I say we spill the beans already."

At this Granddad guffawed and gestured at the Conch. "OK, OK, let's all put our packs in the house, spruce up real quick, then head right back out. The lab is just down the way, and boy do I daresay you kids are about to see the creation that will make everyone's days into straight up the greatest of vacations of play."

Everybody popped into the Conch and plopped their packs down in their respective rooms, all of which flowed into a coalescing coastal show of nautical art pieces lit aglow by the abode's floor to ceiling windows.

After everyone rendezvoused in the kitchen with eyes wide from the home's 360-degree horizon view of the ocean blue, snacks were grabbed as they headed out the back down the garden path along a forested shortcut to the lab.

Satellite sang to herself quietly as they all conversed breezily amongst themselves, taking in the sights of the grandparent's island life. She exchanged an eager expression and a twinkling wink with Isla, Ionakana and Florian. She knew the secret was called the Erusaexel Suit, but beyond that, she could only make her best guess. Whatever it was, Granddad had deemed its release to the world's scene best done with her song and first seen as a music video motif. Satellite bubbled happily as she watched her family and friends trek the neat nature trail to the unveiling.

Suddenly stimulated, Satellite sized up the situation and spoke up. "So, I'm guessing this thing we're about to see is that classified job you guys took that is the reason I'm spending the summer with the grandparents," Satellite directed at her parents. "How come I had to be left in the dark on what my own family is doing?"

Mr. Sacavage looked over his shoulder. "Satellite, this product is a world changer. If any word of this had gotten out in any way, people could have done dangerous things to us to get to our work."

Satellite nodded solemnly, reassured by how her family cared for her, and continued walking.

The trail opened up to a large clearing where the lab sat, sensibly fenced in with key card access to the functional-looking structure. Granddad opened a gate in the fence and everyone stepped through with fresh zesty pep.

A moment later, the main entrance was keyed to a green light, and they all popped inside to where the temperature felt like ice.

Satellite's eyes dashed happily over the absolute future of the huge room. Waving a hand at the vast array of complex technological instruments, Granddad proudly exclaimed, "Welcome to Omnikinetica's top secret retreat! Satellite, with the last-minute help of your parents' expertise on this enterprise, we have completed the finishing touches and had test pilots thoroughly run the product through its paces."

"Test pilots?" Satellite said in shock. "What on earth do they need test pilots for in a suit?" Satellite thought.

"Yes, test pilots," Granddad said feeling very pleased. Granddad beckoned to everyone and led the way deeper into the lab's depths.

A minute later, they arrived at a tall opaque glass showcase.

Granddad, Grandmother, and Mr. and Mrs. Sacavage all stood beside the tall opaque glass showcase and faced Satellite, Florian, Isla and Ionakana.

"And this," Granddad said positively radiating with happiness, "is the Erusaexel Suit."

He flicked a button and the opaque glass cleared immediately to straight transparent. The four friends erupted in "oohs" and "ahhs", smiles spread ear to ear at the searing image of the suit that had given the grandparents and parents a tear.

A muscular mannequin was donning the most designer inspired form-fitting all white item ever contrived. Hooded, with a visor, it was like a slim and trim spacesuit crafted for athletics.

Granddad flipped another switch and just to their side a whole row of opaque cases became transparent panes. Neon pink, acid lime laser green, cherry red, turquoise, sunshine gold, liquid silver, royal purple, matte black, and a tasteful tangerine orange suit splashed all their eyes.

"And the secret," Granddad deliberately looked at each of the four friends in turn, "is that they fly."

Drop-jawed, Satellite, Florian, Isla and Ionakana were dumbfounded.

"What? What do you mean they fly?" Satellite inquired.

"I mean they fly," Granddad said, plumb chuffed as comprehension dawned on them all stronger and stronger.

"These suits are meshed with particle displacement technology we developed back in Switzerland at the CERN particle collider," Mr. Sacavage added happily. "They generate a force on the very fabric of reality, which creates lift and speed. The hood has a cerebral reading system, so movement is controlled by thought. The visor sees and feeds the onboard artificial intelligence providing the flyer with environment recognition and all your safety needs."

"On top of all that," Mrs. Sacavage brightly supplied, "They have a global positioning satellite, or GPS locator, microphone for communication, world-wide internet connection, and a camera built into the visor lens."

"Also," Mr. Sacavage said, tagging on to what his wife was saying, "the self-sustaining battery runs on the same technology as the propulsion, so it has an infinite lifespan."

"And we think the best way to release the Erusaexel Suit is as a music video motif to your song," Granddad said looking with such love at Satellite.

"I… this…" Satellite stammered.

"Like I said, world changer," Mr. Sacavage said.

Satellite looked over at her friends and found Florian's fine face full of the fabulous magic of the Erusaexel Suit's ingenious presence. Florian looked straight into Satellite's soul, and they both knew how big a hit this music video was going to be to unfold.

"When are we going to fly these for the shoot?" Satellite asked looking back at her family.

"First thing tomorrow morning. We need footage sunrise to sunset," Granddad said with a matter-of-fact tact.

The four friends nodded, still in a state of shock, still goggling the designer lines of the suits' full body.

"Well, I say we whip up a light dinner back up at the Conch," Grandmother said warmly taking in the still starry-eyed surprised state of the four friends. "And you kids need to decide which color you want to wear."

Satellite, Florian, Isla and Ionakana turned to face each other, forming a tight knit circle. "Satellite, you're lead, what's your pick?" Florian asked. "Honestly, I'm going with stark white," Satellite said smoothly.

"Oh my gosh, dibbs on pink! I wanna be babed out!" Isla bubbled.

Ionakana chuckled at his sister. "I'm grabbing lime green," he said squinting in his super slick style.

Florian thought for a second, then looked at Satellite. His gaze lingered for a moment, then lit on the turquoise tiger tooth necklace.

"Turquoise," he said, stately. Satellite smiled.

Dinner was a winner that evening. The secret of the suit was out and everybody was in full flow, full glow, as they all rolled over all the beautiful intricacies of the suit's show.

"Just so you know," Granddad said heartily, "there are seven hundred islands and cays in the Bahamas. I daresay you all will have plenty of playground.

"I think establishing shots at sunrise and sunset as introduction and conclusion would be good," Mr. Sacavage said smartly.

Granddad nodded in agreement.

"I was wondering what you think about using some of our footage from our Hawaiian adventures as a prelude to the suits in the video," Satellite asked Granddad. "The first verses of the song could be our cliff flipping clips and skate rips. Once the chorus drops, we introduce that establishing shot of all of us getting geared up in the suits. Then boom! We're off!" Satellite finished with an eager grin.

Everybody liked this idea, and over the dull roar of the dining room Granddad looked at Satellite and said, "For sure," with a grin.

Far from big city lights, the night sky was alive with the sight of the stars' tight white life so bright. The four friends found themselves pushing aside long palm fronds as they made their way off the short trail from the Conch to the sandy stretch of Wade Bay, where a brisk ocean breeze bathed them in the full moon's silvery rays.

"Goodness gracious, I love the beach at night. There's bliss in looking into the abyss," Isla commented calmly looking out over the gently lapping waves of the bay.

Bundled up comfortably in baggy hoodies, Satellite, Florian and Ionakana smiled with their eyes at the infinite night sky.

"Hey Satellite, good idea about using our Hawaii footage as a prelude to the suits for the video," Ionakana said. "God, what a shock it's going to be when we take off. People are going to freak out."

"All these puzzle pieces are fitting together so perfectly,"

Florian spoke aloud to the sky. "Meeting you guys at Starnectar, making 'Smile of My Mind's Eye', having it blow up, sailing to the Caribbean, getting ready to shoot the most revolutionary music video of all time. I am psyching out of my mind right now on all this."

"Mmm... these past few weeks I have been loving life more that I think I ever have before," Satellite mused musically. "And you know what?" She continued, "I am so glad we are filming this music video and showcasing the Erusaexel Suits over islands. The Earth is so beautiful, but islands are just absolute glittering, scintillating jewels atop the primordial truth of the ocean blue. I will say that I'm excited to see all the wondrous locations that these suits will open up for people."

"Geez, those suits are so frickin' awesome!" Ionakana burst out. "I can't wait for tomorrow!"

In a moment of youthful unity, the four friends stood shoulder to shoulder with just their toes in the warm moon-illuminated sea and gazed out, knowing they were about to do a real good-looking one for the history books of fun.

After the sea had granted them each the dreams they wanted to see, Satellite, Florian, Isla and Ionakana huddled together and headed back up the path to the Conch where they could hear the distant blast of Granddad's laugh.

Everyone was in the zone, tucking in for the night nice and clean in the nautical themed bedrooms of the Conch, as the ocean home looked out over the star-studded nightscape of Wade Bay's beach where the full moon roamed all alone.

Pajama clad and feeling wind-swept and mind-blown, Satellite walked to the kitchen for a glass of water all by her lonesome. She stood in the silence, sipping her water, enjoying the quiet, thinking about the shape her future was taking and the amazing way it was lining up so right.

Satisfied with the steps she had in front of her, she padded back down the hall. Just as she was passing the linen closet, Florian emerged from his room, and slightly surprised, halted in the hall in front of her. The fragrances of body wash and shampoo wafted over her.

"Glass of water?" Florian said pointing at Satellite's hand. "Me too."

They gazed at each other, and in their aloneness, they both felt their hearts palpably pounding.

The moment was like a mountain.

Florian smiled, "Big day tomorrow. Sleep well, Satellite." He leaned in and placed a blissful kiss on her smooth beautiful forehead. As Florian padded peacefully to the kitchen, Satellite slipped into her room and gently closed the door. Head spinning, with butterflies in her stomach, she let out a little "Whew!"

In the darkness, she looked skyward through the ceiling and thanked life for today. Feeling complete, she climbed into her cozy bed, got snug as a bug in a rug, and drifted easily off to sleep.

With Blue Island basking in the cool night, the noosphere of the place couldn't have been clearer for all those in the Conch as the riveting future drew so near.

Chapter 9
Zooming Through the Music Video Shoot

"Satellite, it's time to wake up!" The bedroom door was ajar in the dark, and Satellite could hear the sleepy stirrings of the others as her mother leaned over her, whispering her awake.

Through the curtains she could see that the sun had not yet risen. "Day of," Satellite thought to herself excitedly as she popped out of bed, her mother quietly closing the door as she left Satellite to dress in private.

Breakfast was cereal, yogurt, juice and coffee. Everyone was still waking up, with murmurs of good morning and hushed but happy back-and-forths.

Granddad came into the kitchen looking very Caribbean with khaki shorts, a colorful button-up, and a big straw hat with an exotic feather in the thatch that matched his shirt's palette blast.

"OK everyone, let's get a move on. We're going to step down to the lab, get suited up, cover the safety basics, then meet my trusted cinematographers at Wade Bay for the take-off establishing shot.

Satellite, Florian, Isla and Ionakana finished their breakfast, cleaned up, then gathered at the back door. When the parents and grandparents were ready, they all once again headed out and down the garden path through to the forested short-cut, all the while smiling under the still starry night sky.

Through the fence, through the main entrance, and into

the lab they all went.

"OK kids, choose your suits," Granddad said smoothly as he unlocked the glass showcases. With complete confidence, Satellite nabbed the designer white while Isla procured the pretty neon pink, Ionakana lithely lifted the acid lime laser green, and Florian fashionably grabbed his theme piece of joyful boyish turquoise.

After stepping into side rooms to get fitted into their new suits, which, to their liking, slipped on as lovely as a glove, the four friends rejoined the parents and grandparents in the middle of the lab to cover the basic safeties they needed to have.

Mr. Sacavage addressed Satellite, Florian, Isla and Ionakana while his eyes masterfully took in the incredible image that the Erusaexel Suits elicited. "Now, when in flight you MUST have the hood up and visor secured over your vision. The hood's cerebral reader combined with the onboard artificial intelligence's live video feed from the visor is the brain of the operation. While in flight, the system creates propulsion buffers between obstacles in the environment. It is nigh impossible to collide with something."

Satellite, Florian, Isla and Ionakana nodded.

"These suits are capable of pretty much anything you can think for them to do," Mr. Sacavage continued. "Aerial maneuvers, speed, fixed-position hovering, you name it. Be reasonable though. G-forces can knock you out, which in that case, the suit slows to a halt mid-air and waits for you to regain consciousness."

The four friends nodded again, this time with raised eyebrows, as they imagined the kind of flying that would knock you out.

"Any questions?" Mr. Sacavage asked. The suited group looked at each other.

"I'm ready to do this," Satellite said seriously. Florian, Isla and Ionakana steadily agreed in earnest.

"Let's take this party to Wade Bay, baby!" Granddad exclaimed with hands raised.

The sky had a soft glow a moment later as they stepped onto the sand of Wade Bay, where they spotted the camera crew waving them over.

The parents and grandparents cruised over to the side while Granddad pointed at the sky saying, "All right you all, stay in the Bahamas. Remember, the suit's maneuvers are as malleable as your minds make it."

Grandmother, a little choked up, stood fully charmed with her arms crossed and said in a lovely hushed gush, "Finally we have flight…"

The parents nodded encouragingly, giving fresh determination to the four friends as they strode to the middle of the bay's beach to meet the camera crew for the take-off scene.

"OK Satellite, JettySet, and friends, let's have you guys form a circle, spread out, back-to-back, for this establishing shot," the director called out loudly. Satellite took her position and looked over at Florian, who in full JettySet mode, squinted back confidently ready to activate and go. The siblings stood squarely in the sand and shot Satellite a solid stare, raring to blaze off into the air.

The sun was literally a minute from cresting the horizon. "OK you all, we're rolling!" The director yelled as a red light blinked on the camera. "We're going to swoop a few loops around you and as soon as the sun crests, I'm going to yell, 'action!' and then you all flip up your hoods, secure your visors, and blast off!"

Satellite stared straight ahead, ready to absolutely jet set.

The camera crew fluidly moved a few smooth loops around the Erusaexel Suit troupe. Just then, the sun rose over the horizon and shot its first ray of the day into Satellite's glimmering gaze.

"Action!" yelled the director.

Satellite flipped up her hood and fastened the attached visor like a latch. She looked straight up into the sky, and the suit's cerebral reader read her mind as fine as that first ray of light.

Flight.

Satellite was off like a rocket, lifted by nothing but the purity of freedom in her mind.

She loosed a scream of delight at the suit as her mind started flying her higher. Her long-standing sense of reality shattered in an instant as her thoughts began to race with omni-directional possibilities.

Like a dancer's pirouette, Satellite twirled into a swirling vertical spiral and her little girl burst forth like a burning pearl.

"Yo Satellite!" Florian yelled into the mic like a euphoric schoolboy. "Shoot out straight! Let's island hop!"

Precisely as she imagined it, she executed a perfectly tucked front flip then blasted out after Florian.

"Yessss!" Ionakana bellowed like a berserker as he high-fived Isla, who was flying with pride in a straight line.

The four friends tag-teamed for the lead as they tore across the sky, all the while snagging angles of each other as their visors captured all the action, recording the most rip-roaring music video of all time.

Satellite upped the speed with glee, spurring the spree, as they approached the next island scene where all the shores were bordered by clean, pristine beaches.

"We're dropping low! Follow me!" Satellite belted out.

Moving like quicksilver, they ripped down to the rolling ocean and skimmed the shimmering surface with purpose. They were so low they could taste salt and run their hands over the streaking crystalline reefy deep as they bobbed and weaved between each other atop the sea.

In a flash they fired from the deep to the shallows to the beach and swooped like sparrows through the narrows between the breezing palm trees. As they darted over the garden-like island, Satellite spotted a small town.

"Over here! Let's blow some minds!" Satellite got out in a giggle over the mic.

Satellite, Florian, Isla and Ionakana blazed razor sharp in an arc above town and heard the shrieks of people in the street losing their minds as they looked in the sky and saw with their own eyes the never-before-seen sight of the group in flight dressed to the nines in the Erusaexel Suit's fine designer lines.

The four friends flew on without a word of explanation to those below.

"Florian! Let's form some formations and gain some elevation!" Satellite shouted out.

They all flew forward, forming a square in the air while jetting towards a cloud. In an instant, they were inside the cloud surrounded by a soft rainbow illuminating their pop color suits.

"Oh my God, what a shot!" Isla shrieked in elation as they elevated. With a poof, they passed happily through the cloud and blasted laughing into the atmosphere.

"Everyone throw a corkscrew loop!" Satellite sang as the cloud's rain drained off her. The team beamed off in four different directions while twisting blissful corkscrew loops. Zooming their corkscrew loops out of the blue, they formed back up as smooth as you can do.

"I'm taking lead! Diamond up behind me! I've got an idea!" Satellite said as she turned her head and watched Florian, Isla and Ionakana form diamond points behind her. The four friends flew the Erusaexel Suits for all they were worth, as they scorched the skies above the Caribbean earth. They flew high, as Satellite guided the flight above the divine sights of paradise.

Satellite checked the map on display on her visor. "Just over here guys, were going to do it on 'em today!"

Florian, Isla and Ionakana followed Satellite as she flew straight at a city that was a sparkling speck in the distance.

Ionakana checked his map. "Nassau? We're headed to the capital?"

"This is our day," Satellite replied. "Follow my lead."

They blazed straight into the city, Satellite taking point.

"Oh yo, this is going to be sick," Florian said into the mic, very much amused, as Satellite swooped right into the middle of the crowded downtown Nassau.

"Oh my God!" screamed all the bystanders as the four friends flew in and landed light as a feather, clean as can be, smack dab on the white lines on the clean street.

The commotion was a clamor of tumultuous bewilderment, as all the people out in the street tried to make sense of what they were seeing.

Satellite, still at point, motioned with her finger and strode her designer white suit in a glowing full show down the road.

Cameras were snapping from all directions as the awestruck mass gathering came to their senses and started clapping. "Good heavens, what on earth are those?" inquired a drop-jawed man.

"Erusaexel suits. You'll see them in stores soon," Isla bubbled as she bobbed after Satellite.

Satellite proudly wound down the crowded downtown streets with Isla and Ionakana taking flank, and Florian following a few footsteps behind. Feeling a little famished from the flight, Satellite spun on the spot and asked, "Fish taco?"

Ionakana licked his lips while Isla nodded looking around, and Florian unsheathed his head from the suits' hooded visor. "Yes, let's," Florian said happily amidst the continued attention of all the onlookers.

"Visor down, fly boy. We're still filming," Satellite said with a cheeky wink.

They found a seaside seafood restaurant and seated themselves outside at a table where they could see a serene scene of the sea.

"Sooo, this is legendary," Ionakana said, reveling in his acid lime laser green suit.

"I feel like a superhero movie star in a video game that just won the lottery," Isla said saluting the sky with a chic tweak.

"I think the magnitude of how much these suits are going to illuminate everyday living is just starting to dawn on me," Florian said, laughing in acknowledgement at Isla's statement.

"Honestly, I think something like this is an inevitability. I'm just plum chuffed that Granddad and my parents were the ones to make it happen, and here we are, the quad squad, releasing the dream to the world as a MUSIC VIDEO! To our own homemade song!" Satellite said, patting Florian's tan hand on the table.

Four fresh fish tacos later, and the friends were filled up and ready to kill another thrilling flight through the skies.

"Flight ideas?" Florian asked Satellite.

"You bet," Satellite said. "I'm thinking slow, low-flying shots to really stir the island up hot."

Isla giggled. "Satellite, you've got a flair as wild as that crazy red hair."

Satellite smiled while her friends appreciatively beamed at her. "Everyone set?" she said steadily. Three proper nods were the response.

"Boom, let's do it."

Hundreds of heads looked up as Satellite, Florian, Isla and Ionakana lifted off from the front of the seaside seafood restaurant and began slowly roving low through the salty streets. With everyone outside staring up in shock at the sight of their flight in their suits so bright, the four friends flew fluidly through the newly enlivened streets, smiling down kindly from their height.

"Let's go poke around by the boats!" Satellite spoke into the mic as they floated over an old home.

They soared over the shore and swooped a zooming loop through the cruise ships in the large harbor.

"Ooh! Lighthouse!" Isla shouted out.

"Copy that, let's line up and wind a tight spiral on it!" Satellite said spotting the nearby lighthouse. Flying in a single file line, they shot over to the lighthouse and snagged a rad spiral around the tower to the "oohs" and "ahhs" of some tourists that looked on in awe.

"Yo! Let's streak over and take a peek at the marina!" Ionakana yelled, as his visor gleamed in the sunshine's yellow glow.

They streaked over to the marina and carved like sharks through the masts, as those in the dockside bars went from mellow to pell-mell in alarm.

Satellite did a flip, head-over-heels, and hung upside down, hovering, with one hand clutching her stomach, as she squealed like a little girl and gave a thumbs up from up under.

"Oh geez! These are just the bee's knees!" she wheezed, feeling extremely pleased.

Florian flew over to Satellite, flinging a misty flip, and linked arms with her at the elbow. Surprisingly in-synch, the two smoothly started shuffle-step dancing in a right-side-up, up-side-down entrancing fashion that was enhanced by the little flash of romance between them that had been burning since the smash at Starnectar's bash.

Ionakana onlooked with a textbook shot of the dancing duo. "That dance is definitely going in the video," he said as Isla flitted over, putting an arm on his shoulder and her other hand on her heart.

"Oh my gosh! They should totally get together," Isla told Ionakana with her baby girl face hopeful at the dancing duo's soulful show that was rolling over and over still in a hover so low.

Satellite and Florian righted themselves, shaking to their suit's seams with laughter. For a solid moment, they looked into each other's eyes through their visors. Satellite knew she liked Florian, and as she looked at him, she knew he felt the same way. She wanted more than just friendship, but she also wanted their vibes together to be natural and to flow truthfully with their endeavors as artists in collaboration.

They both smiled at each other.

Florian gently placed a hand on her waist and guided her sight to the siblings, who were watching with soft acknowledgment.

"All right you two twitterpated love birds!" Ionakana called out playfully.

"Ionakana! Let them be!" Isla scolded.

Satellite had a hint of a blush on her cheeks, but she fiercely turned back to look at Florian with a wink and a smile that showed all her teeth, "I will say, that turquoise sure does look good on you," she complimented coyly.

Florian chuckled, "You know, you in that designer white; you really fit the description of the pop star you're about to be."

Satellite smiled, "This is fun; you and me, I mean." Florian rocked a nod, "I think so, too."

"You guys talkin' 'bout make-out techniques or what? Let's get a move on! I'm dying to fly!" Ionakana ployed with pomp.

Satellite and Florian flew over and joined back up with the siblings while Isla gave her brother a few frustrated slaps.

"Honestly, I say we do a free-styling, free flowing, free form towards home," Satellite said taking charge again. "We're in the heart of the Bahamas with islands on all sides. We can island hop all the way back to the Conch."

Ionakana clapped his hands while Isla looked out in the direction of Blue Island, and Florian sighed serenely at the other three hovering above the sea.

"Free-styling, free flowing, free form? You could have just said go crazy!" Ionakana chided lightly.

Satellite laughed, "That works too."

At that, the four friends took off in a blast.

On the flight back to the Conch, they knew full well that all the loops, shoots, flips, dips, wild island spirals of time wiling, cloud chopping, block walking, crowd cheering, seafood eating, and entrancing dancing enhanced by Satellite's and Florian's romance was all a staunch nod to the Sacavage family entourage and the suit and song product that was about to skyrocket launch.

Satellite flew without a care, meandering through the air, aware that their fabulous island flight was going to get edited into nothing short of a nuclear bejeweled visual for all the people to reach for and cling to forever more.

The beauty of the Bahamas beneath them was truly boggling as they all goggled in their tag-along gaggle. As they breezed above the sea, they breathed a deep sigh of relief as they spotted the Conch from afar atop its hill on Blue Island overlooking Wade Bay with its beach.

"Granddad, come in Granddad, do you copy?" Satellite called over her mic.

"Granddad here, I read you loud and clear," Granddad said in response.

"We're approaching Blue Island, are we landing on the beach at Wade Bay?" Satellite asked.

"Copy that, that's an affirmative," Granddad said happily. "Nice and easy does the trick, make it a very conclusive landing to end the flick. Boys start rolling! They're coming in!"

Satellite laughed at Granddad's authoritative but excited commanding of the camera crew on the land.

Satellite, Florian, Isla and Ionakana swooped through into

Blue Island and started hearing cheers as they cleared a sheer veer near to Wade Bay and dropped in low and slow to close the maiden day. The young team landed just peachy on the beach while the camera crew snagged the shot, capturing with their apertures, the scene like paparazzi chasing celebrities.

"Well?" Granddad asked as he practically bounded across the beach, meeting Satellite and her friends three.

"Oh my God," Satellite said whipping her wrist as she blew a chef's kiss signaling her exquisite bliss at their trip. "The flying felt like velvet, and boy did we melt into it when we started telling the suits to belt it out and really pelt the skies with all the bells and whistles of these missiles that you guys designed," Satellite frothed, as her mom and dad brought Grandmother to the party the suits had started.

"Oh, Satellite dear," Grandmother said happily with a hint of a tear of joy in her wise eye, "I'm so glad we put you at the pivotal point of these suits. You're a darn good darling for people to see living the dream."

Everyone gathered chuckled with laughter, appreciative of Satellite's red-headed smashing panache.

Satellite looked to her parents who were gazing proudly at her on her momentous day.

"You did a real fine job out there," Mr. Sacavage said serenely.

"If you want to do the flying," Mrs. Sacavage said softly, "you have to keep your mind clear cut like a diamond. And that's exactly what you all did, nice and wild, with grace and style."

"Let's get you kids out of those suits, my crew is going to have a field day with all that footage you all got today," Granddad said. "And," he continued, looking at Grandmother, "the ladies cooked up a good dinner for everyone tonight, what was it now?"

"Shrimp Alfredo with bread and asparagus," Grandmother and Mrs. Sacavage chimed in chorus.

"Boom, there you go," Granddad said, "let's all head home to the Conch. I've got another big surprise I want to talk to you kids about."

At that, the Sacavages escorted the Erusaexel Suit troupe back to the Conch in the best-day-ever mood that they were vibing to like Satellite's bop of song that was now coming true.

Dinner was a delight as Satellite, Florian, Isla and Ionakana recounted their flight. They all went into great detail on their tale, with everyone getting a kick out of their prevailing Nassau fly-over sail. As Satellite wrapped up their blast, Granddad leaned in seriously.

"OK now, time is of the essence here. The music video will be ready soon, and will be released to the world shortly after." Granddad looked at each of the four friends in turn, finally focusing in on Satellite and Florian.

"Your song represents the unveiling of the Erusaexel Suit and the album you made carries that feeling forward. I want to do a world tour to promote the suits in person to live audiences in twelve major cities. I think a three-hundred-and-sixty-degree concert from atop twelve skyscrapers, with all the pre-order people in those cities in attendance, is the skyrocket docket we need to show people that this really is the hottest product to ever drop."

Satellite was drop-jawed.

She looked over at Florian, who was also beyond awestruck. "I'm in! I am so in! Are you in?" Satellite said to Florian.

"Ab-so-lutely in," Florian said, straight to Satellite.

"Isla and Ionakana too, right? They're my backing vocals!" Satellite asked Granddad.

"Yes, everyone. I can have this green-lighted tonight. You all just have to want it," Granddad said.

"YES!" The four friends said in unison.

"Done deal," Granddad said heartily. "And that's a wrap. You kids get some rest. We've got some jam-packed weeks ahead. I want to see everyone at one hundred percent."

Sleep that night was deep as they all reeled in their sheets at their dreams that were now real.

Chapter 10
The Hottest Globe Trot to Ever Drop

The next handful of days were a montage of memorizing the songs of Satellite's album. Many an hour was spent drifting around Blue Island with a speaker on blast, as the four friends chanted the charming lyrics complimented by the bionic banger tracks of Florian's chord progressive palette attack paths.

In between rehearsals, Satellite, Florian, Isla and Ionakana became very well-versed on competing in beach relays to tighten up their physiques before they stepped into the global spotlight so everyone could see them at their peak.

They also squeezed in some tandem adventures in see-through canoes atop the breezy ocean blue, with Satellite opting to go with Isla around the island so they could talk girl to girl in truth.

"You ready for this tour?" Isla asked Satellite once their transparent canoe was out of sight of the boys who had gone on ahead around to the right.

"Absolutely. These songs are me and everything I believe in," Satellite said. "And with Florian on music and you and Ionakana backing me, we can for sure smash every one of those twelve cities."

They had a fantastic paddle around the island, and as they all regrouped and ambled up the path from Wade Bay to the Conch, Granddad called out to them from the upper porch, where he was perched like a hawk.

"All right you guys, hope you're ready to see some real magic happen," he said. "The music video is slotted to premiere tonight during primetime. And to strike while the iron is hot, we are booked solid in all twelve cities, starting tomorrow night in Miami atop the Panorama Tower."

"Ho-ly mackerel, we are about to get so lit," Ionakana commented confidently in awe.

"Now our flight is just after midnight, so let's all get packed up and be ready," Granddad added.

Satellite, Florian, Isla and Ionakana spent the afternoon doing laundry, packing, and straightening up while excitedly exchanging whimsical wishes about quick activities to do while in each of the cities they were going to visit.

By the time the music video for "Smile of My Mind's Eye" with the Erusaexel Suits was slated to show, Satellite was positively as bright-eyed and bushy-tailed as some number one bunny in a glade in the vale.

The grandparents, the parents, Satellite, Florian, Isla and Ionakana were all gathered in the Conch's living room chatting, and then, right on cue, a boom loomed as the JettySet track blasted off in a plume.

"Good Heavens!" Grandmother exclaimed as the video opened with Satellite's gargantuan gainer off Spitting Cave.

"Whoa!" Isla and Ionakana chorused together as quick clips cut briskly by from their Oahu trip.

Satellite's voice was just as otherworldly as always, searing all their ears with its seemingly infinitely deep reach as everyone peered at the T.V. screen with glee.

Then the establishing shot at Wade Bay popped up.

Just as the sun rose over the horizon, the chorus erupted,

and the four friends in the Erusaexel Suits rocketed off.

"Ohhhhhh!" Everyone cheered at the perfectly timed unveiling of this future to the world, knowing full well that the world was watching drop-jawed and awestruck.

The color of the suits, the blistering speed as they blew through the blue sky with their tubular moves, the beauty of the Bahamas, and the raw originality of the straight fire song; it all made for the tastiest eye and ear candy they'd all ever seen and heard.

As the last riff glistened against their eardrums and the sunset shot faded to black, Granddad's phone lit up.

"Wildfire," Granddad stated smiling, checking his phone. "Orders are going through the roof. Guys, these concerts coming up are going to be crazy."

"That was an incredible endeavor on everyone's part," Mr. Sacavage said brightly as he leaned back on the Conch's couch, putting his arm around his wife.

"Satellite, Florian, Isla, Ionakana; you just made the first impression image and sonic memory for something that will one day be a staple of daily life," Mrs. Sacavage said sagely. "Hands down all around, you all should be proud."

Satellite spent the next few hours talking about what this new future was going to look like, all the while shooting glances out the sliding glass doors, eager to pour forth her heart and soul into the world tour.

The much-anticipated time rolled around, and Granddad jovially called to them all from the kitchen where he had wheeled his gear. "Time to fly to Miami and get this party started!"

"Yep! We're ready!" Satellite called back.

The four friends popped into their rooms and lugged their

luggage into the kitchen where Satellite did a last-minute rummage, then gave the thumbs up. "Good to go!" she said fast and steadfast.

"Oh, leh do it!" Ionakana burst out.

"Picture of the sun, yeah we hot right now," Florian abstractly added with a flashy smashing gesture.

Isla simply did a little booty groove by her suitcase and cooed, "Let's get a move."

Granddad nodded and started for the door.

"What about Grandmother and Mom and Dad?" Satellite asked.

"Your grandmother isn't up to hit twelve cities at a lightspeed pace. She'll be glued to the tube, don't you worry; she won't miss your shows. And your mom and dad didn't want to leave her alone," Granddad leaned in with a wink. "You didn't really want your parents to be present as you party like an animal, did you?"

Satellite thought it over for a moment then chuckled, "Well, as long as they catch the concerts on T.V."

Granddad nodded again with a knowing glow. "Everyone squared away? Let's go!"

The drive across the island was quick. Everyone was in high spirits as they slipped into the jet for their first leg of the trip. The flight was a solid power hour of hype as the four friends sang Satellite's songs high up in the night sky.

In no time they landed at Miami International Airport and shuttled over to their hotel where they spent a few hours sleeping well.

"Up and at 'em!" Satellite chanted rousing her tousled-hair companions.

Brunch was a blur as they all had omelets and coffee at a

124

restaurant in South Beach across the street from the pristine sea breeze scene.

"All right you all, we need to be at Panorama Tower nice and early to run through everything," Granddad said. "They helicoptered the speakers up last night; the biggest baddest ones there are," he added happily. "Oh, and Florian, they brought up DJ equipment through the roof top service door; all you'll need is your laptop."

Florian smiled, patting his pack. "Dang, Mr. Sacavage, this is insane. I'm ready to play the waviest set ever." He looked at Satellite then looked back at Granddad. "Thank you so much for putting all this on."

They left the restaurant and loaded up in the Lamborghini Urus that Granddad had rented as they contentedly went to the event.

Upon their "Ooh" and "Ahh" arrival at Panorama Tower, there was a block-wide flock of people waiting outside. Still a shock to see, pre-order people were already flying gently in their new Erusaexel Suits around the tower, looking like sour candy specks in the sky as they waited for the concert to ignite.

Satellite stepped out of the Lamborghini onto the sidewalk and was immediately spotted by onlookers that were goggling at her red head amidst the hot knot of people on the block.

"Yo! You're Satellite, right?" A teenage boy asked, hurrying forward with his phone.

"Oh, yeah!" Satellite said smiling. "That's me!"

"Yo, that song is a banger! And it's a JettySet track! Oh, yo! And there's JettySet!" he said, noticing Florian walking around the Lamborghini. The boy snapped a quick selfie with them just before a swarm of photographers, media people, onlookers, and even a few in Erusaexel Suits clustered in on

Satellite, Florian, Isla and Ionakana.

The time span between their arrival at Panorama Tower and the concert was handshake after handshake, and a steady stream of meet and greet with fans and famous people alike right there in the Miami street.

Finally, the time arrived.

The four friends were gently jostling in the tight spot just inside the roof-top service door when Granddad popped in behind them.

"All right you guys, good luck out there," he said. "Remember, this is a celebration of a new form of freedom with the songs of Satellite's soul at its heart singing. Keep yourselves unfettered and soak up the pleasure of performing."

Granddad patted each of them on the back, checked his watch, and then said, "Boom! And the cannon blasts!"

At that he opened the door.

Satellite was struck by the sun as she saw the sunset casting its warm colors on the hundreds and hundreds, nay, thousands, that had flown up to the top of Panorama Tower in their brand new Erusaexel Suits for the concert. The cheers were ear-splitting as she stepped out.

A hand closed on hers and she looked over to see JettySet looking back. "We're on," he said.

Smiling, they nodded at each other.

JettySet flew to his suspended DJ rig while Satellite, her suit's mic linked to the huge rooftop speakers, flew forward with the siblings behind her and to each side, their chests out in courage.

"Hello, all you suited-up super tune groovers!" Satellite sang out in her enchanting voice.

"YAAAAAAHHHHHHH!" The airborne audience yelled

back. Satellite smiled bigger than she ever had before.

JettySet flicked a switch and "Smile of My Mind's Eye" erupted like a volcano over the speakers. People were bobbing and weaving, hovering, flying all around, and just straight up being free as Satellite's song seared all their ears with its visions so clear.

Satellite, JettySet, Isla and Ionakana performed all fourteen songs in the album all the way from "Sea Spray Face" to "Creature Comforts".

As the last chord sounded long and strong then faded, the airborne audience screamed with everything they had.

"Oh, my starry-eyed surprise, sundown to sunrise, we gonna dance all night, dance all night!" Ionakana belted out at the freshly popped stars.

Sure enough, that's exactly what they did. Satellite, JettySet, Isla and Ionakana hit up pretty much every after-party in every club and danced all night right there in Miami's famous nightlife.

Now that Satellite and the gang were activated in the eyes of society, their trans-Atlantic flight was nothing short of absolute magic. They landed in London, heaved their stuff into a hotel, then got straight to some tourism.

They saw Big Ben, the Crown Jewels, rode the London Eye, lunched on fish and chips, then toured the Harry Potter movie studios.

"Yo, Harry Potter is like my favorite book series of all time," Ionakana proclaimed as he passed through a group of Potterheads. "On the real though, those books make you feel so good," Isla tacked on as Ionakana chatted with the Potterheads steadily.

Dinner was bangers and mash at a somewhat grubby but

lovable little pub. "I like the whole British etiquette and mannerisms, they're so proper," Satellite commented over the commentary of two nearby up-standing but somewhat sloshy blokes.

Florian chuckled, "Yeah, I vibe with that kinda royal boarding school thing that England is famous for."

They finished up at the pub, and as they made their way to the venue for the night show where they were about to explode like a supernova, they saw a few handfuls of Erusaexel Suits flying above the twilight London skyline.

That night, Satellite, JettySet, Isla and Ionakana rocked lava hot atop Twenty-two, one of London's most prominent high rises.

"We're switching the set list! Gotta keep it fresh!" Satellite yelled over at JettySet and the siblings. They punctured the night sky with "Pop Out Atop the Canopy", with thousands of people in Erusaexel Suits shining with the life of flight.

The four friends felt like a family amidst the familiar flashing lights and laser foray as they played the rave crazy JettySet tracks on blast, with Satellite's gorgeous other-worldly voice making the crowd feel that super amazing way straight to their face.

Paris was next.

Granddad made sure they all got a full night's sleep, but first thing that next morning, they visited an outdoor café for espresso and pastries where they were spotting more and more people popping up amongst the population in brand new Erusaxel Suits.

"All right, you kids, time is tight. Let's move this tour to the Louvre," Granddad guided lightly.

Satellite smiled, "Man, we are straight charging! Let's get it!"

Granddad and the four absorbed as much of the historic culture as they could at the Louvre Museum, appreciating each of the artist's attention to aesthetics. They did have a schedule to keep, so at some points they were practically dashing like mad in-between works to see all there was to be had.

They had a bit of a late lunch of bread and cheese while sitting on the grass of the park with the Eiffel Tower towering above them, where it cut the sky so sharp.

"Well, no time to dilly-dally, let's get you all to the show so you can lead this Parisian rally for another city on the tally," Granddad said standing up.

"Whew!" Satellite said brushing back her berry red hair. "Florian, you've done a world tour before, how did you adjust to such a tight schedule?"

"Oh, I live for the fast-paced life. Being an action-packed savage is pretty fun," Florian casually replied with a bright laugh.

The Paris show was a late afternoon boom with the four friends kicking it off with "True Views from a Blue Moon". From an outsider's perspective, the top of the Tour Total building was simply a swarming orb with the rainbow of suits coursing like whitewash on a stormy shore.

As the airborne audience applauded after the concert and took their raucous partying to other rooftops, Ionakana mimed twisting a thin moustache and said aside to just Isla, "Ah, Pari, zit iz ze zity of looove," then busted out in a chuckle.

Isla looked around and saw Satellite and Florian hovering extremely close to one another, talking heart to heart. She smiled.

Satellite and the gang kicked it to Madrid for the next blissful mission on the hit list.

"You know we bout to get it on some Spanish cuisine!" Ionakana exclaimed as they all walked and talked up and down the intriguing streets.

They tucked in at a little local spot and had huevos ritos, pincho de tortilla, bocadillos de calamares, soldaditos de pavia and cocido madrileño.

Afterwards, they were able to catch a bit of a midday fútbol match.

"You know, looking out at this match, it's only a matter of time before the Erusaexel Suits spawn a sport of their own," Florian reckoned.

Satellite perked up.

"Oh yes, that thought did occur to my developers that enveloped the cultural impact of the suits as they move humans into the future," Granddad said smoothly.

"Oooh! What else do you think the suits will start?" Satellite inquired.

"Well, new jobs for sure. Since the suits are self-sustaining and clean, they'll make a dent in the transportation industry. I'm betting on new art forms, games, technology; like I said, they're a world changer, a shining icon of a new zeitgeist. The very foundation of daily living is getting reinvented," Granddad said proudly over the loud surrounding crowd.

The sunset show that evening atop the Torre Cepsa building was nothing short of a sanguine celebration of solid Spanish salud.

Satellite blasted off with "Passion Fashion" which really animated the immaculate Spaniards. As her enlightening voice opened the eyes and enlivened the minds of all those in flight, fireworks started rocketed off across town casting even more color on the high-altitude multitude as sunset changed to twilight.

Satellite and the gang's escapades had escalated them into an overnight earworm sensation that was stunning nations with fascination at JettySet's orangutan bangers and Satellite's angelic vocal exhalations.

The four friends were feeling like absolute fire as they roamed through Rome. They did find time to grub on some lunch at a local eatery where they had pasta carbonara, pizza al taglio, suppli, and saltimbocca.

"I literally feel like we're sprinting for glimpses," Isla remarked as they all snapped shots at Trevi Fountain.

"This is what it's like living the star life in the world's eye," Florian said lightly.

"Yeah..." Isla breathed, "who am I kidding, this is awesome."

Exuding neon vibes, they hiked around the Pantheon for the sights to the excitement of passersby who now recognized them with hype. They absorbed more culture as they breezed through the Colosseum, The Sistine Chapel, St. Peter's Basilica, and the Galleria Borghese. Florian even flicked a coin into the water at Piazza Navona; "Never pass up a chance to make a wish."

The show that night atop the Torre Pontina building was a bedazzling razzle-dazzle for the packed crowd that encapsulated Satellite, JettySet, Isla and Ionakana as they started smashing with "The Laughing Path".

No sooner had they rocked Rome that they found themselves in Cairo, Egypt visiting the pyramids of Giza.

Time was tight, but they did manage to peruse the bizarre bazaar and purchase some authentic keepsakes of Egyptian art.

Practically mid-stride, they had a snack of koshary, fuul, taameya and kofta kebabs as they saw it all from a rooftop spot. "Half-way mark, stay sharp," said Granddad who was with them today.

"Man, the skies these days seem to always have some suits zooming through them," Satellite said with her eyes skyward as some young Egyptians shot overhead, smiling as they overheard.

"They're going to get the world going bananas," Florian chuckled. "Yeah, but man, they go straight hammer," Ionakana said, smiling at Florian like a rascal.

Satellite serenaded the sunset that evening atop The Grand Nile Tower Hotel, kicking it off with "Lifted in Glyphs", which the airborne audience, old to the kids, sang word for word, lit to the hit.

After a day of spa, sauna and massage, the entourage was ready again to get it on. The Moscow show was mayhem as JettySet dropped new massive mastodon bombs that sounded body builder strong and really made the throng's minds get gone as they gushed to the Russians atop the Naberezhnaya Tower till dawn.

The stoic Russians really loved "Don't Look Away", and despite the freedom of flight, they were a very square-jawed solid crowd all the way into the morning light.

After a much-needed nap, Satellite, Florian, Isla and Ionakana discovered for themselves the iconic, colorful, onion-topped photo backdrop of St. Basil's Cathedral.

"Always wanted to see that," Ionakana said gazing at the cathedral. "Kinda funny lookin'," Isla commented.

A little later they sank into some savory pelmeni with sides of shchi that they had heard were must-tries of local eating. Through a mouthful, Ionakana managed to get out a "Yo. I can't wait to finish this global hot-foot-hopscotch and get home so I can walk down a Kauai country road with that fat paycheck in my pocket."

Isla looked affronted, "Ionakana!"

Satellite held up a hand, "Nothing wrong with that. Granddad is going to pay us handsomely. This is a blast, and it is my passion, but it will be great to successfully put this tour in the bag and kick back and relax."

Airport, jet, airport, and they were in the mix for another night of lasers, lights, flight, and music so hype as Granddad and the four friends woke up in Singapore and set straight to striving to make their show strike even more right.

Streaming along, they snacked on satay on skewers then visited the only spot they had time for, The Gardens by the Bay, with the alien trees that loomed over them.

"Now, this is what I like to see," Satellite said, as the troupe trooped through the heart of the garden. "A super future blend of space-age structures and the lush love of a jungle touch."

"Yeah, I feel like I'm in the greenhouse of some kind of satellite space station in orbit," Florian said looking over at Satellite as they all explored through another door.

Their afternoon show was an absolute riotous flight atop the Marina Bay Sands Hotel SkyPark as they started off with "Sunshine Science" with the shiny city's skyscrapers monolithing the horizon.

Unconcerned, mid-concert, as they all surged above the Earth, Satellite suddenly felt a dark dearth. It felt like the cerebral reader had passed a feeler over her, momentarily stifling her control and cheer. It was only for a moment, and in the midst of her performance, she was forced to shrug it off.

Yet something had definitely passed over her.

While they were on the jet to Tokyo, Satellite found a moment to slow the roll and question the unknown.

"Did any of you all feel something weird from your cerebral reader?" She asked.

"Nuh uh,"

"No, all's good,"

"Mine's as clear as a bell," the three replied.

"Huh, maybe it was nothing…" Satellite said pushing the thought away.

"What's this now?" Granddad asked, looking over from his work.

"Oh, I dunno, maybe it was nothing. I thought I felt the suit's cerebral reader pass over me with a darkness for a second," Satellite said.

"Hmmm… We've had a zero percentage of glitches in the system. I'll have someone run a diagnostic to check it out just in case," Granddad said reassuringly.

Satellite was back in her zone as she stepped foot in Tokyo with Florian, Isla and Ionakana who were already in their suits, hones and toned, for the show that now felt like home.

They all graced the cityscape that was a high-tech mecca of ultra-aesthetic tastes.

As soon as they were spotted, the floor was lava as they popped from spot to spot with Erusaexel Suit mobs going instantaneously insane at Satellite and the gang's alchemy.

As Satellite cruised smooth through Tokyo under a sky so blue, with a cloud of proud Erusaexel Suit troopers to boot, she thought to herself how clean the city was as she toured for views.

Setting down for a second, Satellite, Florian, Isla, Ionakana, and the huge group of fanatical youth in suits savored some sushi sitting in the setting of Ueno Park; a place famous for people getting in the scene of the cherry blossom trees.

"Tokyo's got that bright light vibe I like," Satellite said, amidst the gargantuan gathering they had amassed in passing.

"Agreed. And this sushi is the bomb dot com," Florian said happily as he laughed at some Tokyoite teens flying through the trees that lined the path.

That night they ravaged like savages atop Roppongi Hills' Mori Tower, escalating the ear drum exhibition with "Electro Escape" as the first-place song to race across everyone's high attitude, high altitude rave game face.

Satellite, Florian, and the twins saw the sun rise next morning at 38,000 feet as their jet soared towards the sunny shores of Sydney, Australia.

With not a second to spare, Satellite pony-tailed her raspberry hair as they had a same-day show atop Greenland Centre that was for sure going to attract half the people along the coast.

"Yo, Aussie's got that earthen aura," Ionakana commented as he unapologetically gawked at a flock of hotties.

Satellite and Isla smiled while Florian let a whisper of a wink ping the scene.

Clean and dripping with style in her designer white flight suit that was now a worldwide motif piece, Satellite beautifully rampaged with "Bathing in the Cascade" atop the tower to a behemoth loud crowd as a certified teen dream living in the hearts and ultra-vibrant to all eyes with a desire to see.

Isla and Ionakana were having such a blast, literally laughing out the backing vocals of every track to the open local folks whose totally noble socials were focused like coated opals as they stayed mobile.

JettySet smashed out new jackhammer attack after jackhammer attack, as fresh wet and wild waves of sound crashed on his dashing tracks.

The Sydney show was a scintillating success, and afterwards they burned with an outstanding excess of energy as they gave post-show interviews with the press.

Satellite and the gang managed to grab a bite of barramundi with avocado toast, spot the Sydney Opera House, and raise a toast to the most as they bounced off the Australian Coast.

"Land of the free, home of the brave! Back in the good ol' USA!" Ionakana exclaimed half a day later as their jet touched down in Los Angeles International Airport.

They had time to kill, and Satellite could think of a whole list of thrills, so the four friends suited up, stepped out, and took off filled with chill. The sky was buzzing with an absolute flooding of clubbing Erusaexel Suit troopers as Satellite, Florian, Isla and Ionakana dive- bombed the Hollywood Sign for a fire photo from a fellow flyer.

"We're going across town for a bite!" Satellite called over the mic. Minutes later, they were nibbling on clam strips on the Santa Monica Pier. "Frick me, I love America," Ionakana said contentedly after finishing his strips.

"Yeah man, and LA has a certain magic to it. It's like everything is glossed in movies," Florian commented honestly to Ionakana.

"Well, now we've got some sauce from all across a globe trot," Satellite said. "Truth is better than fiction; we have real lives that hit and leave 'em sizzling."

The friends laughed while Isla snapped a selfie as they sat by their empty clam strip helpings.

They filled the rest of their day by blasting by the Griffith Observatory, touring over Universal Studios, arcing over a park and landing on the castle in Disneyland, flying by Rodeo Drive, sharking down Sunset Boulevard, perusing over the zoo, staring down at the aquarium, hodge-podging over the Dodgers, and catching some trill vibes over the Hollywood Hills.

After a solid night's deep sleep and a breakfast that kept them lean, Satellite and the three flew down the street for their mid-day concert atop the U.S. Bank Tower in the city of the silver screen.

With a breezy steeze, Satellite bowled the whole show over with "Star Soul" rolling out as the four friends hit go.

The thousands in the crowd had a certain famous flare as they swarmed the skyscraper in a sphere with Satellite's red hair going everywhere up there.

Another show, another city, another blessing of Satellite's otherworldly voice igniting minds and lifting people up so pretty.

JettySet enjoyed a moment looking at Satellite there atop the tower surrounding by a crowd treating her like a flower and said to himself, "God, that chick is it!"

After a cross-continental jet set, they landed in New York City for the final leg of the tour that had the whole world airborne with a style that was statuesque.

Straight from the jet to the top of Freedom Tower, they were about to finish their global song spree strong, starting off the night with "Smile of My Mind's Eye" ready to play with loud power. It was a huge glowing show and it seemed like a quarter of the city was present there, pouring forth towards Satellite at their core.

"Good evening, boys and girls, ladies and gentlemen, I'm Satellite, that's JettySet," she gestured at JettySet at his DJ rig, "and these are my friends, Isla and Ionakana. I hope you enjoy my songs, and I hope you enjoy the suits. I'm going to kick it off tonight with a tune guaranteed to put you in a good mood."

Right as the music started and rolled over everyone's eardrums like a boulder, Satellite inhaled, ready to sing, when suddenly the cerebral reader grabbed a hold of her mind with a darkness so deep, she couldn't even see.

To the screams of everybody on the scene, her suit pulled her down, forcing her to plummet off the Freedom Tower towards the street.

Chapter 11
The Seraph

"Satellite!" JettySet screamed.

"Grab her!" Ionakana yelled.

JettySet, Isla and Ionakana razor traced the space between people and pelted after Satellite's plummeting body.

They were flying top speed straight down, but so was Satellite's suit.

The deadly concrete of the street was nearly upon them. With inches to spare, the three got their arms around Satellite and curved out, but at their speed, in the traffic lined street, Satellite's hand smashed out the back window of a car and with a sickening pop her left wrist broke.

"Slow her down, slow her down!" JettySet yelled.

But despite all three of them trying to bring Satellite's speed down, her cerebral reader was going haywire and was unrelenting.

JettySet and the twins lost their grip, and Satellite slipped away shattering through a third story window where she wrecked her way through the office space, bowling over desks, chairs, and fabric-covered cubicles then smashed out the glass headfirst on the other side.

"What are we going to do?" Isla shrieked with a tear streaking down her cheek.

"We have to catch her and rip her hood off! Her cerebral

reader has taken control of her!" JettySet yelled out as they flew around the building looking for Satellite.

Easily spotted, she was scraping up the side of a skyscraper looking beaten up and bloodied.

As they jetted towards her, her suit skyrocketed off the skyscraper, shooting straight up.

"Oh my god! Gun it, you guys! We gotta get to her!" Ionakana desperately yelled.

Satellite's suit was shooting straight up through the airborne audience of thousands above Freedom Tower, where she slammed her way through countless people who were torn on how to handle her.

Satellite, severely hurt, was barely conscious, with her body locked by the cerebral reader's pitch-black dearth as she rose higher and higher above the Earth.

The artificial intelligence in the suit had completely overcome her; she couldn't hear, see or feel; all her being was darkness.

The suit had sensed something in Satellite, something that was only present in her and her alone, and it was trying to read it. Only it was something unreadable, and the cerebral reader was going crazy trying to make sense of it.

Satellite was so high in the sky now that it was getting cold. To make matters worse, oxygen was getting low too.

"We have to get to her!" Ionakana yelled in a hoarse voice as his chest heaved with the difficulty of breathing.

JettySet, Isla and Ionakana were close to Satellite who was still shooting skyward, but the lack of proper oxygen was causing their lungs to hurt.

In a moment of terror, Isla's head lolled over sideways as she fainted from the lack of breathable air.

"Ionakana! Grab your sister! Take her back, I'll go on!" JettySet managed to bark out in the dark.

Ionakana whipped around wearily and grabbed his twin sister safely in his arms with his eyes bleary from tears.

JettySet took one last ragged breath as he closed in on Satellite down to an arm's breadth.

He had so little oxygen in him he could barely stay focused, and his strength was down to one last throw.

Climbing Satellite's beaten and bloodied body, with his arms too heavy to reach up to her hood, his life came to one final move.

As his last breath left him, he pressed in and kissed Satellite on the lips with all the love his life had ever known, all in one rushing gush as their lips touched.

Satellite, feeling that final sword brandish as JettySet's life force hit her lips and vanished, wrenched her mind more violently than she had ever imagined, and a divine beam of light exploded in her and blazed like a blazar from her eyes.

The cerebral reader, which had been seeking to read the unreadable, read the divinity of Satellite's beam and its control over her fell short of her otherworldly glory.

Satellite, looking through eyes that were not human, lifted JettySet's chin as he drifted out with barely a whisper left in him.

With a soul from another world looking out at him through its pretty little red-headed avatar and its ethereal aura that was exuding mind-bending gleans of infinite angelic things, the soul spoke to him, igniting his mind like they were the last two of their kind at the end of all space and time.

"Florian Faleafine, you have saved a seraph of reality. You will be rewarded in all you do in this universe and in all that follow."

Florian froze, realizing what Satellite really was, then passed into unconsciousness.

"Wade Bay really is quite a gem," Satellite thought to herself as she looked with ocean eyes at the bay from the porch of the Conch.

It had been a blurry few days.

She had hazy memories of darkness, pain, a kiss on the lips, a fire in her mind, carrying an unconscious Florian down to a swarming press frenzy, faces looking on in shock, a trip to the hospital, and a vague jet flight back to the privacy of Blue Island.

Her body was all beaten up; black and blue, through and through.

Florian, Isla and Ionakana had all been rushed to the hospital as well, then afterward flown home to Hawaii.

Satellite looked at her arm that was now in a cast. Some kind of miracle had happened up there in the air. And something now shone brighter than ever in her.

"Oh Satellite, there you are," Grandmother said gliding out the sliding glass doors onto the porch.

Granddad and her mom and dad came out too looking with concern at Satellite standing in front of the view of the ocean blue.

"Satellite, I am so sorry that happened to you," Granddad said. "You are the only reported case of a cerebral reader going haywire. The only things I can think of that could make a reader do that is if you had an absolutely alien brain that was completely unreadable; or maybe there was something that the A.I. wanted to read but was incapable of comprehending."

Satellite looked at her family, unblinking, with a microscopic Mona Lisa smile.

"Whatever happened up there in New York," Granddad continued, "we have put a cap on how far the cerebral reader can go inside a mind. This should never happen again."

"You really can't remember what happened up there?" her dad asked. "Because that situation, in those conditions… you were physically within an inch of… of… losing your life," her dad finished with his voice caught in his throat.

"Something must have kicked in last minute," Satellite said.

"And it doesn't help that she's going to turn straight around and go off to one of the hardest colleges in the world," her mom said, looking at her.

"What? I got in? I got into Kaimana Hoku?" Satellite exclaimed, forgetting all her pain.

Her whole family nodded at her warmly and assuredly. "When do I start?" Satellite asked happily.

"Pretty darn soon," her dad said. "It's awful that you had to get so badly beat up before your first day of school," he sighed, "but I daresay you'll fit in just fine. Heck, the whole point of that school is to turn out superstars, and you're showing up already a full-fledged celebrity." He winked.

Satellite glanced over her shoulder at the ocean for a moment. The moment rose as Satellite's hopes went up.

"And you guys?" Satellite asked, looking back at her family. "What are you guys going to do now?"

"Well, we plan on flying too!" her mom exclaimed, shaking her raspberry mane.

"Yeah, and we're all ready to start work on Erusaexel 2.0," her dad said, looking at his dad.

"Yep, you guys know how technology is. Second it comes out, people already want the next thing," Granddad said, winking.

"Oh deary, you are going to have so much fun in college," Grandmother said. "So many bright young minds. And you'll have plenty of time for all that you want to find."

Satellite thought of Florian, Isla and Ionakana.

"You know, I think Florian and I would make quite an item," Satellite said with the eyelids on her pretty little sphinx visage fluttering in the sun.

The family's concern disappeared as they all flashed big smiles that stretched from ear to ear.

Just a short week later, Satellite was on Hawaii's Big Island at Kaimana Hoku School of Visionary Consciousness. Being a freshman, her first semester looked a lot like the visions she had glimpsed from the turquoise tiger tooth necklace: uniforms and drill formations; a lot like a boot camp. It was going to be tough, but she was ready for the challenge. Plus, she'd get a dorm next semester with a roommate; an experience she was looking forward to.

She was still pretty beaten up, but in great spirits as she walked across campus, backpack full of books, to her first class.

Suddenly, something caught her eye.

Looking like a million bucks in his turquoise Erusaexel Suit, Florian was striding toward her.

"Florian!" she shouted out.

"Hey Satellite. Heard through the grapevine you'd be here. Just wanted to wish you good luck on your first day," Florian said smiling while he looked her up and down then rested his eyes in hers.

Satellite laughed. She was happy.

"Hey, in all seriousness," Satellite said with an extremely cheeky eyebrow raised, "you wanna be my boyfriend?"

"Babe, I am all yours," Florian said with no hesitation, putting a hand on the small of her back then leaning in.

They shared a beautiful kiss right there, smack dab in the middle of campus.

"How are Isla and Ionakana?" Satellite asked as their lips parted.

"Couldn't be better. They're over on Oahu at The University of Hawaii at Manoa, starting school, same as you."

"Oh!" Satellite said with a start. "I know it's not much, but I have little tokens of our friendship I'd like to share with everyone." She rummaged through her backpack and extracted the chimera figurine and handed it with a smile to Florian. "I've got some for the twins too, just a knick-knack for the bedside table," she winked.

Florian appraised the chimera appreciatively for a moment then said, "Thank you. You know, we're all only a short flight away from each other. We can switch who visits who on weekends," Florian smiled. "Tell you what, we can get a jump start on one of your school projects by going ahead and starting your much-anticipated second album."

Satellite laughed spectacularly.

Touching the turquoise tiger tooth that she still had on, Satellite and Florian each grabbed a bottle of Granddad's lilikoi juice from the campus store, then strode boldly to her class with divinely lit eyes that shone through and through; true.